SCOEFIELD

BY
NICHOLAS M. KROHN

1

Dedicated to my heavenly Father, God Almighty,
My Lord and Saviour, Jesus Christ,
And His cleansing and gentle Holy Spirit.
I thank Him for the salvation He has given me, the
innumerable blessings within my life, and allowing my
dream of being an author to come to fruition. I pray that
this novel is glorifying and honoring to Him.

3

TABLE OF CONTENTS

CHAPTER ONE

How do you ask someone to do something you know they'll say no to? That's an odd way to start a book, I suppose. In truth, this book is intended for someone very dear to me. However, I don't think he'll ever read it. No one may ever read this book. I don't know. I'm not even certain of how I should write this. Should I write it like the reader already knows what happened? Or should I explain everything just in case the reader doesn't know? Well, if I were to do the former, this would be a very short book. So, I'll write it all. Hold on to your seats. I may go a little fast.

My name is Henry. Henry Engel. I am twenty-six years old and the date is July 25th, 1943.
And I am German.
Well, in all technicality, I am an American citizen from birth. My father was American, but I was born in Germany. Bonn, Germany. I'm not sure how you'll view me, considering Germans don't exactly have the best reputation as of late. I would ask you to simply put away such discriminative feelings, if you have any. I am human just like you. And, if it is to help the case of my people, Germany and Nazism are not synonymous. I don't believe that all of the people of Germany are caught up in some hellish cult. Many, maybe. But all? I don't think so. For the most part, though, I can't say. I can't because I do not know for certain. I just believe Germany is deceived by a madman. Yeesh, look at me, I'm already getting off track. You can see I love Germany, can't you? My father went to Germany in 1913, wanting to be a missionary to the German people in World War I. Pretty ambitious, huh?

Probably the worst war that has ever taken place thus far, and my father heads to Germany. Not with a gun. Not with a sword. Not with a plane. With a Bible. My father wanted to start a church in the midst of chaos. He met my mother in 1914, and two years later, my parents met me.

Henry Arvin Engel, born December 17th, 1916. My father told me often how I was the sign of the end of the Great War. World War I ended around two years after I was brought into this world. But Germany had a high price to pay. They committed several war crimes, for which most of the world was very angry. My parents didn't quite tell me what the soldiers of Germany did, and I was content with not knowing. Some atrocities are best left unspoken. For these crimes, Germany was imposed with severe reparation payments, lost significant amounts of land, had to take full responsibility for starting the war, was only able to have an army limited to 100,000 men, was not allowed an air-force, and so on and so on.

Germany was hit hard by such punishments. Being German, I must say that I believe that some of these punishments were unjust. To pay for the repair of entire nations, such as France, was far too much to ask. Germany was not able to handle such monumental debt. Some believe that the fire of World War II began to kindle directly after the Treaty of Versailles. The treaty, in most German eyes, was nothing but a shame and cruel judgment. Anger was clenched in nearly every German fist. But not my father's. My father, Franklin Engel, trusted God with unshakeable faith. My mother stood directly beside him with similar trust in the Lord. Even when Germany fell into a depression, they remained faithful to God. Even when money was little, they remained faithful to God. Even when the church had to be closed, they remained faithful to God. Even when we had no place to live, they remained faithful to God. Even when we were without any material possession, my parents remained faithful to God. That's why I believe so fervently in God. Because my parents showed me He was real. We had nothing in a country that was struggling to survive, yet God was taking care of us. I had no toys to play with, yet we were given food every week. Just by "coincidence", we would happen to come across food somehow. God was still there, He was answering our prayers, keeping us safe.

And when all hope was gone, God made for us an escape. A letter arrived for my father. It was from my grandfather.

Now, before I continue, I believe some other things need addressed. To whoever may be reading this, there is only one person that this book is truly directed to: Bradley Leonard Scoefield. My best friend. Of course, he would never allow me to call him "Bradley". He says "Bradley" is a pathetic name. To everyone that knows him, he's simply "Scoefield".

Scoefield, I don't know if you're reading this, but if you are, you can probably skip all this explanation. You know it already. I don't know, maybe you'll want to read it. To be honest, it's refreshing for me to go through all of the memories. It might be for you, as well. Correct me if I get anything wrong.

Dear Franklin,

What do you think you are doing?! The church tells me you are living on the streets! Son, your wife and your child are suffering because of your stubbornness! Come home, boy. Come home to New York. Do not worry about paying for the trip, it is already done. America has been doing very well. I will take care of you and your family. You will get a job here and, when you are financially secure, I will let you go back. You do not have to, though, Franklin. You are so far away. Maybe you are supposed to be here to take care of your elderly father. And who knows? Perhaps Germany needs some time to recover. We have much to discuss, but none of that needs to be done now. Just come home and we can work things out together. The tickets for the zeppelin should be with this letter. I paid for first class. You can thank me later. Enjoy the flight.

Sincerely,
Your father.

My parents didn't want to leave Germany. I, however, was torn. It would be nice to stay, but, let's face it: life was horrible. I, being only a child, did not have the discipline and faith my parents did. I wanted a nice bed to sleep in, a full serving of food, shelter from the harsh weather. After some discussion and prayer, my parents decided to go to America. It would just be for a little while, they told me. Father would get a job and save up money so we could come back someday.

On September 2nd, 1929, we left Germany for New York. And I received everything I had wished for.

See, my grandfather was rich. He lived on a large estate out in the country. I was given a bed that was large enough to hold seven children. I was given so much food that I could hardly finish the appetizer. As for harsh weather, it never

reached within the strong walls of my grandfather's house. I was happy. Especially when I got to do something I had never heard of before:
Fishing.

"So, are we providing dinner tonight, *Großvater*?" I asked my grandfather as we fished on a nearby lake.
"Boy, what did you just call me?"
"*Großvater*." I repeated. "It means-"
"Son, you are in the glorious United States of America. The magnificent land of freedom and capitalism. So, speak American."
"American, Grandfather?"
"That's right."
"Don't you mean English?"
"English is for England." Grandfather told me sternly. "Do you call cookies 'biscuits'?"
"No."
"Do you say 'bloke', 'jolly good', or 'Yankee Doodle'?"
"Grandfather, Yankee Doodle isn't British."
"Sounds British enough." Grandfather argued. "Either way, you understand my point?"
"Yes, sir."
"Now, what was your question?"
"Are we providing dinner for tonight?"
"Oh-ho, my dear boy." Grandfather chuckled with a gleam in his eye. "Let your grandfather teach you a thing or two about how your life will be here. Have you ever fished before, my son?"
"No, sir."
"How do you think of it?"
"It's…foreign."
"Foreign? Explain, son."

I shrugged my shoulders as I stared at my pole. "I've never done something like this. In Germany, we were always doing something. Something that was hard or productive or…something like that. We never sat around and was rewarded with fish because of it."

"And that is the glorious thing about fishing, my lad!" Grandfather guffawed. "You sit and wait and have a good chat while the fish contemplate about snatching that lure of yours."

"I suppose that is rather nice." I smiled. "It's been nice ever since I arrived here. Just waiting for food to come to us. God is good to give us fishing."

"God is good, my boy!" Grandfather cheered. "But we're not having these suckers for dinner."

I was confused. "We're not?"

"No, my stomach can't handle fish." Grandfather told me. "They disagree with me. No, we're having a good, hearty steak for supper!"

I blinked at him. "Steak sounds nice…but if we're having steak, then why are we out here?"

"Well, I like to fish."

"You like to fish but you can't eat fish?"

"You are correct."

"What are we going to do with the fish when we catch them?" I quizzed.

"Throw them back." Grandfather stated.

"Throw them back?" I gaped. The idea of ripping into a fish's lip, dragging it out of it's environment, yanking the hook out of it while it's suffocating, and then tossing it back seemed rather savage to me. It would be like shooting a deer in the leg, running up to it, chopping off it's antlers for a keepsake and then letting it go.

"So, we're doing this for fun?" I asked after a long pause.

"Somewhat."

"Oh?" I inquired.

"I am also out here with you, Henry, because I do not know my own grandson." He smiled at me. "And I would very much like to get to know you."

I felt something deep within me grow warm. Warm like the rays of the sun coming out from behind stormy clouds.

"You took me fishing because you wanted to get to know me?" I marveled.

"Of course, Henry." My grandfather assured me. "We are family. All that I have is yours, and believe you me, I have quite a lot. Trust me, my boy, you'll never have to beg or be in want ever again. You now live with Lemuel Engel. Anything you want, it's yours."

"I don't need much, sir." I said quietly.

"Pish posh! You'll have it all!" Grandfather argued. "Money is no longer an issue. Now, Henry, tell me about yourself. Let us learn of one another."

We didn't catch one fish that day. Not a single bite. But it didn't matter. I was able to talk with my grandfather and really bond with him. I told him of my time in Germany, my dreams, my convictions, and so on. In return, he recalled to me his hard childhood of poverty and how he promised himself he would become very rich so as to never suffer from lack again. And he did so. Now, with investments in many stocks and such, he was doing extremely well. And he was more than willing to share it with my father, my mother, and me.

Everything was going wonderfully. My father got a job. And while Grandfather and I were out doing things together, Mother would either tidy up around the house, go shopping, or meet with some new friends she had made at our church. She was taking it a bit harder than Father and I, being away from her home country. But she wasn't complaining and she was adjusting to this place called America.

At the American church called Bible Baptist Church, I began to make friends as well. There was a boy around my age named Charles. He had come to America from England and had a wonderful British accent. I suppose that I had a German accent, though I couldn't really tell. Everyone in America seemed to have a sloppy-sounding accent. Charles himself actually laughed at my accent. He said that my 'th' pronunciation was hilarious. There is no 'th' sound in German. So, instead of saying 'the, their, and them', I would say 'ze, zeir, and zem'. Charles often told me how I always sounded like I was hissing or that my voice was breathy. I would retort with saying that his language had no 'r's, for he would always say 'ahh' instead of 'are'. My favorite thing to say to him was 'The art at the mart will make you dart from your cart as your heart will rip apart'. Charles would say 'The ahht at the mahht will make you dahht from your cahht as your hahht will rip apahht.' I loved it.
And then we would both make fun of the American accent by noting how lazy it was. 'T' and 'd' were basically identical. For example, in 'medal' and 'metal', the 't's and the 'd's sound exactly the same. 'U's were useless in some words, and vitally important in others. Like in 'caught' or 'purpose', the 'u' doesn't have to be there or it doesn't even sound like a 'u'. Yet, in words like 'ruin' or 'mule', the 'u' is quite necessary.
Strange, isn't it?

The American language wasn't as difficult for me as it was for my mother. Mother was talking about how she found it rude that people would make fun of her because she didn't pronounce 'w's right. She would make a 'v' sound instead. Instead of 'why, where, and when', she would say 'vy, vere, and ven'. Anyway, I'm getting off topic. The point is that I was starting to adapt to America. Slowly but surely, Mother was as well. Our Pastor at Bible Baptist Church was very friendly and hospitable to us. His name was Wayne Benson. His sermons were powerful, his counsel was faultless. Every Sunday I would find myself walking away with a new wonderful truth about the Bible or it's Author.

Unfortunately, Grandfather didn't enjoy coming to church. He hardly came with us. However, Grandfather and I did something different every other day. One day, we went driving in his fancy car. Another day, we were eating ice cream. Another day, we were going to watch a baseball game. Wonderful and crazy days those all were.

And I loved my grandfather.

I really really loved my grandfather.

But one Tuesday morning, after breakfast, Grandfather got a telephone call.

We were supposed to go fishing on that day.

My grandfather collapsed, clutching his chest.

I didn't understand what was happening, but the stock market had crashed. Grandfather had lost everything. And Grandfather's god was not the Lord, but money.

Again, I am not speaking ill of my grandfather. I loved him. He cared about me and he was a great man.

Grandfather died of a heart attack on October 29th, 1929.

CHAPTER TWO

LEMUEL C. ENGEL

1867 – 1929

A funeral. The first one I had ever been to. We couldn't afford a large or fancy tombstone. But we made due. The feelings that ran through me were feelings of confusion, pain, and regret. Confusion because I didn't know why something so simple as money would cause my grandfather to lose his life. Furthermore, it didn't feel like he was gone. Pain because he *was* gone. Regret because…well, I'm not quite sure. But I felt there must have been something that I could have done. Something more.

Father did his best to keep the family strong. We inherited Grandfather's house, though we had to sell nearly everything he had. We managed, however. Father was able to keep his job. Things were going to get better, so it seemed.

But something in me never felt quite right after that.

I became more of a quiet person. I used to talk little. After Grandfather's death, I didn't talk at all. Mother and Father were becoming worried. They weren't sure what to do. What do you say to someone who says he's okay but truly isn't?

I spent many days talking with Pastor Benson. He assured me that death was a natural part of life, but that didn't make me feel better. If anything, my talks with Pastor Benson only confirmed that my grandfather was not in heaven with Jesus. And that was almost too much for my weak shoulders to bear.

My grandfather was not a saved man.

And that broke my heart.

It made me hate sleeping in his house. It made me despise the sidewalks on which he once walked on. It made me long for Germany. No one had ever died in Germany.

"So, we may never go back to Germany?" I questioned my parents on one afternoon. We were driving to town to sell the car we were driving. Grandfather's car. A rich man fancied it and we needed the money.

"We don't know, son." My father spoke. "For now, we believe God wants us to stay here in New York. After all, the Lord provided me with a good job, even in these times."

"I'll have to go to an American school?" I sighed, disappointed.

"Now, Henry." My mother could see my lack of enthusiasm. "Americans are not all bad. Just look at your father."

My father glanced at her. "I'm not sure if I should take that as a compliment or not."

"You should, darling." My mother laughed. "Americans have many shortcomings."

I laughed with my mother.

My father seemed a tad irritated. "Oh? Like what?"

"They are always ill prepared for the day. They are obsessed with baseball. They have horrible tastes in food." My mother began to list.

"You're talking about *me*." My father tried to hide his smile.

"Yes, I am talking about you." My mother laughed heartily.

"Oh, I'm so sorry I've been such a terrible American husband!" My father shouted sarcastically.

My mother laughed with him and I couldn't help to laugh along. Laughing was precious for me in those days. I didn't do it often.

I loved it when my parents would joke around.

But it was all too short.

Our car was suddenly smashed into by a large truck.

For years, I blamed the truck driver. I claimed that he had hit us by running a stop sign. Although, if I'm going to be truthful, that's not how it happened. My father, distracted because he was trying to make his family laugh, ran a stop sign. Our car was struck on the driver's side. My father died instantly. I remember it very vividly. I remember everything aching as blood ran down my cheek. My head had hit the window and cracked the glass. I was bleeding because I had gotten cut. That was all. I was fine. Nothing major. A little bruised and disoriented, but fine. I was panicking, though. I glanced out the opposite window to see a truck there. The driver was getting out of his car, terror all over his face. Then I saw my father. My father was lying limp against the steering wheel. I began hyperventilating. This could not be. It should not be.

"Franklin? Franklin!" My mother called weakly. I pulled myself over to the middle seat to find my mother. Her head was bleeding far more than mine was. I could tell it was very bad. She looked at me while her eyes were fluttering.

"Henry. Are you all-right?" Her voice wavered.

All I could do was nod.

She looked like she was falling asleep, or about to lose consciousness.

Before she did, she said one last thing to me:

"God is always there for you, *Liebe*. Never doubt that."
And she closed her eyes.
Later on, the doctor told me that she had internal bleeding.
She had not fallen asleep right then. She had died.
I was a lone German in the world of Americans.
Before long, I was preparing myself for another funeral.

FRANKLIN J. ENGEL

1892 – 1929

HEIDE G. ENGEL

1898 – 1929

Those images would be forever burned into my memory. They were buried next to Grandfather. Friends from the church could only afford one tombstone. 1929 became the worst year of my life. In September, I had a joyous grandfather, a wonderful father, and a loving mother. By November, I had lost all of them. Since I had nowhere to go, I was going to live in an orphanage. The next days were a blur to me. What I had gone through with my grandfather's death was amplified with my parents' deaths. Sorrow overwhelmed me like a thick, heavy blanket. It was as if I was in a dream, or hallucinating. That's how those memories are to me now. I only remember a few details: the policeman that tried to comfort

me, the meetings with my pastor, seeing the headmaster of the orphanage. But I wasn't really there. I had just been hit with a monumental tragedy. My parents were gone.
GONE.
The two most wonderful people in the world were taken from me. And I couldn't help but wonder why. Why would God allow it? They were God's servants.
Faithful.
Strong.
Compassionate.
Wise.
Lovely.
But still...gone.

I couldn't cry. My tears had long dried away. It was as if I was now in a world without color, without good. That evil sought to claim me everywhere I turned. The only solace I had to cherish was that my parents were indeed bought by the blood of Jesus Christ. They were with Him in heaven.
That thought saved me from my despair. Still, I remained in that daze for many days. I finally started to come back in tune with reality a couple weeks after I had arrived at the orphanage. It was nice. Nicer than I believed it would be. I would be allowed to go to church and I would be provided for. That was pleasant, I suppose, but I didn't really care at the time. I didn't know what to think. I felt more emotionless than anything. My first undazed day at the orphanage was a good one, though.
"Hey." One kid approached me. "I'm Ralph. You're new here?"
"Relatively." I nodded. "I'm Henry."
"Hi, Henry." He smiled kindly.

"Hi."

"I know you've probably gone through a lot." Ralph could see the sadness in my face. "You want to talk about it?"

"No."

"I understand." Ralph sympathized. "But if you need someone to talk to, just find me. Okay?"

I gave a small smile. True, my life had become quite hard, but at least I was treated with kindness there.

At least for one day, I was.

I didn't yet know the animosity towards Germans. And the next day, I had revealed my nationality with one simple greeting:

"*Guten tag.*" I greeted Ralph the next morning.

It caused quite an atmosphere of tension. Boys all around began looking at me. Some with anger. Others with fear. I didn't understand.

"Why are they all looking at me?" I whispered to Ralph. But then I noticed he was doing the same. He was staring at me with a mixture of horror and sorrow. As if he had just watched me die right in front of him. He quickly ran off as other boys made their way towards me. Older boys. They looked anywhere from fifteen to seventeen years old.

"What did you just say?" The leader of them grunted.

I gulped, very afraid. "I said '*guten tag*', sir. It means 'good m-'"

"I don't care what it means!" He shouted. "Are you a German?"

"Y-yes."

The boy's anger intensified. "My daddy was killed by Germans. They killed him with mustard gas!"

"I-I'm sorry." I started backing away from him. "I...I don't know what mustard gas is..."

One of the boys grabbed my arm, preventing me from backing up any further.

"You making fun of me?!" The leader yelled.

"No, no, I-I really don't know-"

I was interrupted with a violent beating. The others around him helped by kicking me, punching me down, spitting on me. All who didn't get involved stood back and watched. Some nodded or smiled with approval. Others simply seemed too scared to do anything about it. I had to go to bed that night with a bloody nose, busted lip, black eye, and several bad bruises all over my body. The next day, I was called to the headmaster's office. I was somewhat relieved. I could tell him what happened, and he would see my wounds. He would help me.

"You are here to receive disciplinary action for the fight you started yesterday." The headmaster stated firmly, taking a paddle out from his closet.

I was baffled. "No, sir. I didn't start the fight. The older boys just started beating me up."

"Oswald told me you insulted his late father." The headmaster said. "I would do the same if someone had slandered my father's name."

"But I didn't, sir!" I began to cry. "He just started beating me up because he doesn't like Germans! Please believe me!"

"Why should I believe you, German?" The headmaster asked me, giving me a nasty glare. "Germans always lie and they always cause trouble. Now, are you going to take your punishment like an American, or like a German?"

I then realized that I was not in a safe haven, but in a prison. I was violently beaten by a group of teenagers and then punished for it with a paddle to my rear. And the bullying did not end there. My food was taken several times by a variety of boys. No one did anything to help me. No one ever wanted to play with me or let me play with them. I was constantly mocked and insulted for my nationality. Sometimes, older boys would push me or slap me just because they felt like it. If I talked back or tried to stand up for myself, I was beaten again. Then paddled the next day for causing a fight.

I cried every night, wondering where God was and why He had done this to me. I wondered why He had taken my parents from me. Why He had put me in a place that hated me for reasons I could not alter. But every night, when everyone else was sleeping, I was comforted through God's Word. I was not allowed a listening ear, but I was allowed a Bible. And one Psalm spoke to me quite particularly: Psalm 34.

"I will bless the LORD at all times: his praise *shall* continually *be* in my mouth.

My soul shall make her boast in the LORD: the humble shall hear *thereof,* and be glad.

O magnify the LORD with me, and let us exalt his name together.

I sought the LORD, and he heard me, and delivered me from all my fears.

They looked unto him, and were lightened: and their faces were not ashamed.

This poor man cried, and the LORD heard *him,* and saved him out of all his troubles.

The angel of the LORD encampeth round about them that fear him, and delivereth them.

O taste and see that the LORD *is* good: blessed *is* the man *that* trusteth in him.

O fear the LORD, ye his saints: for *there is* no want to them that fear him.

The young lions do lack, and suffer hunger: but they that seek the LORD shall not want any good *thing.*

Come, ye children, hearken unto me: I will teach you the fear of the LORD.

What man *is he that* desireth life, *and* loveth *many* days, that he may see good?

Keep thy tongue from evil, and thy lips from speaking guile.

Depart from evil, and do good; seek peace, and pursue it.

The eyes of the LORD *are* upon the righteous, and his ears *are open* unto their cry.

The face of the LORD *is* against them that do evil, to cut off the remembrance of them from the earth.

The righteous cry, and the LORD heareth, and delivereth them out of all their troubles.

The LORD *is* nigh unto them that are of a broken heart; and saveth such as be of a contrite spirit.

Many *are* the afflictions of the righteous: but the LORD delivereth him out of them all.

He keepeth all his bones: not one of them is broken.

Evil shall slay the wicked: and they that hate the righteous shall be desolate.

The LORD redeemeth the soul of his servants: and none of them that trust in him shall be desolate."

This was a Psalm that some believe David had written when he was delivered out of the hands of a Philistine king named Achish. David had unwisely gone to this king for refuge. He was a known enemy of them, and some Philistines began to recognize him. Had he been truly found out, David would have been executed. However, perceiving that they were beginning to discover who he was, David began to act like he was insane. King Achish saw this display of insanity and ordered him to be thrown out. In truth, I don't think that should have worked, but God was with David, so He mercifully saved David. So, David then supposedly wrote this Psalm, to praise the Lord. And no, my situation was nothing like David's. In David's case, he had just been delivered from his problem, whereas I was yet to be delivered from my struggles. But, it still brought warmth and encouragement to me. It was comforting to know that God listens to those who cry out to Him. So, while in high spirits, I sang a hymn. I sang "What a Friend We Have in Jesus":

"Welch ein Freund ist unser Jesus,
O wie hoch ist er erhöht.
Er hat uns mit Gott versöhnet
und vertritt uns im Gebet.
Wer mag sagen und ermessen,
wie viel Heil verloren geht,
Wenn wir nicht zu ihm uns wenden
Und ihn suchen im Gebet.
Wenn des Feindes Macht uns drohet
Und manch Sturmwind um uns weht,
Brauchen wir uns nicht zu fürchten,
Stehn wir gläubig im Gebet.
Da erweist sich Jesu Treue,
Wie er uns zur Seite steht,
Als ein mächtiger Erretter,
Der erhört ein ernst Gebet."

I sang this quietly, of course. I didn't want the other boys waking up and hearing me sing in German. The German version is slightly different than the English. It translates:

"What a friend is our Jesus,
O, how high is He exalted!
He has reconciled us to God
And intercedes for us in prayer.
Who can say and judge
How much salvation goes lost,
If we do not turn to Him
And seek Him in prayer?
If the power of the enemy threatens us
And many storm winds assault us,
We need not to fear,

24

We stand believing in prayer.
Because Jesus proves to be true,
He stands by our side,
As a mighty Savior,
Who answers earnest prayers."

It was only the first two verses of the song, but I really related with the second verse, and it helped. After all, the next day was going to be just like the last.
Mocked by day. Praying by night.
Stolen from by day. Praising by night.
Insulted by day. Singing by night.
Beaten by day. Worshipping by night.

CHAPTER THREE

I was in torment. I know it sounds like it's more... childish. Calling my time as being bullied like I was in the bowels of hell itself. But it wasn't easy. I was there for three years. And it all started when I was twelve years old. I was orphaned, with no friends.

For three years.

I felt so alone and I was being treated like a criminal. But one November night in 1932, my prayers were answered. I was aroused from my sleep by an older-looking boy. At first, I cringed in fear, believing I was going to get beaten again, but he assured me otherwise.

"I'm not here to hurt you." He whispered. "I'm here to help you."

I was skeptical to say the least. I realized it was a boy named Azarel. I never spoke to him before, nor he to me. This was our first encounter.

"Don't worry." He said. "Grab your coat. I can get you out of here."

"*Get me out of here?*" I thought to myself as I hesitantly followed. I wasn't sure, at that time, that I wanted to actually leave. Yes, I was in a place that I hated, but what awaited me on the outside? After all, I was not fed or given a place to sleep on the outside.

But still, I followed Azarel. We reached the door to our sleeping area, which was usually locked. Couldn't have boys leaving in the middle of the night. However, Azarel took a key from his shoe and unlocked the door. He glanced around before actually opening the door. We snuck out into the courtyard and came to the front gate. Azarel had a key for the gate as well.

"You might as well own this place." I muttered as he unlatched the gate.

"I've been here a while." He replied quietly. He then opened the gate and motioned for me to go through.

I eyed him, unmoving.

"What?" He asked me.

"Why are you helping me?" I questioned. "Everyone else hates me because I'm German."

Azarel was silent for a moment. Then he reached into his shirt and pulled out a necklace. On the end of the necklace was the Star of David. He was Jewish.

"I, too, know what it is like to be judged simply for being a certain nationality." He explained to me. "And I, too, am a servant of Jesus Christ."

"I've never spoken to you before." I scratched my head. "How did you know I was a Christian?"

"You think we couldn't hear you praying at night?" He smiled.

"I pray in German." I replied.

"That doesn't mean we don't know what you're doing." He shot back. "You better go. And good luck."

However wise or foolish it was to leave the orphanage, I left. Into the snowy streets, I fled my place of persecution. I believed it was God that had delivered me from the orphanage, but how would I take care of myself, being all alone?

I pondered on this as I trudged through a thin layer of snow.

"*What am I doing?*" I questioned in my mind. "*This is crazy. I'm going to starve out here. Or freeze to death.*"

But I didn't turn back. I knew that God had gotten me out of the orphanage for a reason. I just didn't know what that reason was and, to be honest, I was rather doubtful and very afraid until…

"Sleep in heavenly peace. Sleep in heavenly peace." I heard a young girl singing. She was singing Silent Night. I spotted her down the sidewalk underneath a street lamp. She seemed about fifteen years old. About my age. She was very thin and fragile-looking. She had long, curly, dark brown hair and a face that looked like it belonged to a China doll. Her nose was rather pointed and her expression seemed to be stuck in that of sorrow. She wore clothes that were far too big for her and didn't seem to be sufficient for the cold weather. Her skin was pale white, almost like the snow she stood in, but nearly every inch of her was covered in a small layer of grime.

For as late as it was, this sidewalk was rather busy. Men and women were passing by her every second, a few of them tossing coins into a little hat the girl had lying at her feet. As I approached, I realized the reason so many people were around was because there was both a bar and a strip joint near where the girl was singing.

That was rather…disheartening. The girl was standing there, singing Silent Night, and people were going to intoxicate themselves and be immoral. But I began to focus on the girl. Every time she finished singing Silent Night, she would begin it again. Start the song completely over. As I watched her sing, I began to ponder if that was the only song she knew. As time went on, more and more people were ignoring her completely. The time between coins flopping in her hat was increasing. Everyone was passing her by, not even looking her way. I could tell by watching the girl that she was very cold. The shivering was in her voice. She didn't have sufficient clothing for

November. Her coat was thin and worn. As I watched her sing, my heart went out to her. I could feel the Holy Spirit nudging me, saying "Help her, Henry."

I had nothing. That much was true. I had just run away from an orphanage. How could I help this poverty-stricken girl?

"*I have no money, Lord.*" I excused in my mind.

My conscience turned on me. "*You don't need money to help someone.*"

"*I can't do anything truly helpful.*"

"*What **can** you do? Stop thinking about what you can't do and think about what you **can** do.*"

I blinked. What I could do.

(Now, just to clarify, God was not audibly talking to me in my mind. That would be rather wonderful if He would do that, but He doesn't work that way anymore. It was more like...you know that voice that speaks to you when you do something bad, like lying? You lie to your parents and then you feel it go "You shouldn't have lied". It's almost like a thought that you don't think yourself. Just wanted to say that. Sorry to slow you down.)

"*Well, let's see.*" I scratched my head. "*She has a beautiful voice, but no one is paying her any mind. Maybe she just needs a new song.*"

A new song. I wasn't the person to ask when it came to that. The only songs I knew were German songs. People didn't appreciate Germans in that time.

"*Well, I do like to write.*" I thought. "*Maybe I can write her a song.*"

All I would need was paper and something to write with. Immediately, I thought of a hotel I had passed on the way here. I ran back a couple blocks to find it. I quickly made my way inside without a moment's hesitation. The clerk instantly noticed me as I approached his desk.

"Excuse me, young man, but where are your parents?" He asked me.

I took a deep breath. It still felt like it had only been a day since I lost them. Whenever people asked me where they were...it was like losing them all over again.

"They're at home in heaven." I told him with a quivering breath. The clerk's eyes suddenly became a mixture of shock and sorrow.

"Do you have a piece of paper and a pencil I could use?" I asked him before he could say anything else.

The clerk seemed very surprised that I would ask such a question. "Um...yes."

He hesitantly took a piece of paper and handed it to me, along with the pencil.

"Thank you." I smiled. "I'll bring back the pencil when I'm done."

"No, you just keep it, son." The clerk told me.

"Thank you, sir."

I quickly ran back outside. Huffing and puffing my way back to where the girl was, I found her still singing Silent Night. I sat down on the sidewalk and began thinking as I scribbled several things on my piece of paper.

"*It will need to be a song that grips people's hearts.*" I concentrated. "*Something that they'll need. That they'll appreciate. That will help them carry on when it seems like they can't.*"

I stopped for a moment.

"*God is always there for you, Liebe. Never doubt that.*"

I took a deep breath. "Mama..."

I began writing. Writing not just for the girl, not just for the people she would sing it for, but also for myself.

Something that would help me to go on even when it seemed like I couldn't.

I finished just in time. The girl had stopped singing and was counting the coins in her hat. She looked like she was about to leave when…

"Excuse me." I called to her and hurried over to where she was.

She turned to me, looking at me as if she was determining whether I was a threat or whether I had money. Her eyes glowed wonderfully. They were a pleasant green, with specks of gold in them.

"What do you want?" She asked, rather rudely.

"I have something for you." I held out the piece of paper.

She looked at it, then looked back at me. "What good will paper do me?"

"You'll have to read what's on it." I told her.

She shook her head. "I can't read."

I was a little surprised, though I shouldn't have been. There were plenty of people that didn't know how to read in those times.

"What's it say?" She asked.

"Oh, um, well…" I muttered. "It's a song I thought you might want to sing."

The girl thought about that. "Sing it to me and I'll see."

Sing to her. I wasn't much of a singer.

I tried anyway. "Oh, uh, okay…"

I looked at the paper as I began to sing.

"I know the struggle.
In your eyes, the pain I see.
How could this happen?
Why would God let this be?

31

Friend, I don't know how I can help.
And I don't know what to say.
But in my heart, I know this truth.
The night will turn back to day.

You're never too lost to be kept from God.
Never too hurt to go on.
Never too beaten to try again.
Never too foreign to belong.

You're never too sunk to be lift up.
Never too far to find your home.
Never too hopeless to find God's grace.
And you are never alone.

Human hand cannot help you.
Money has its limits.
But if you turn to God's Holy Word.
And place your trust in it.

I know you'll never be too lost to be kept from God.
Never too hurt to go on.
Never too beaten to try again.
Never too foreign to belong.

You'll never be too sunk to be lift up.
Never too far to find your home.
Never too hopeless to find God's grace.
And you'll never be alone.

God has not forgotten you.
He will not forsake-"

I stopped singing. I heard the girl crying. I looked up from my paper to see tears running down her face.

"Are you okay?" I whispered.

"Don't stop." She cried. "Keep singing. I want to hear the rest."

"But I-"

"Please." She begged.

I looked back at my paper.

"He will not forsake you.
Lay your life at Jesus' feet.
And though you're going through hardship,
He will make you new.

Stay with the merciful Saviour.
Submit and carry your cross.
You'll lay up treasures you can't imagine.
That will never suffer loss.

You're never too lost to be kept from God.
Never too hurt to go on.
Never too beaten to try again.
Never too foreign to belong.

You're never too sunk to be lift up.
Never too far to find your home.
Never too hopeless to find God's grace.
And you are never alone."

I looked up from my paper again. The girl was nigh weeping. So much so, that she couldn't even speak to me. I felt awkward. I had made this girl cry, but I was pretty certain that it wasn't necessarily a bad thing. When she recovered herself, she began speaking with me again.

"Thank you." She whispered.

"For what?"

"I don't know how to put it into words." She admitted. "I just...really needed that. What is that song called?"

I took a moment to think of a good name.

"Never." I told her.

"Did you write that yourself?"

I nodded.

"It's beautiful." She smiled. "Will you sing it with me?"

"I'd rather not." I commented. "I just wanted to give it to you. I'm not much of a singer."

"You were wonderful." She smiled again. She had a very stunning smile. "Please sing it with me."

"But..."

"What's your name?" The girl asked me suddenly.

"Henry." I told her.

"I'm Sarah." She introduced herself. "Please sing with me, Henry."

She had a beautiful smile, a beautiful voice, a radiant face, precious eyes....How could I say no?

We sang 'Never' on that street corner together. Many people passed by and many stopped to hear our song. Some people cried. Some people seemed to get this fire in their eyes when they heard the words. And we got a lot more than just lose change. We got dollars. After we were done and counted up all the money, we discovered we had forty-three dollars.

Sarah and I just stared at each other after we counted it all up.

"Forty-three dollars?" Sarah gaped. "I've never made forty-three dollars before!"

I didn't know what to say. "Do you have a safe place to keep all of this?"

"Once my brother gets here, he'll keep it safe." She beamed.

"HEY!" A rough-looking boy shouted at us from across the street. "I thought I told ya' boys to stay away from my sister!"

Before anything could be said, the boy bounded across the street like he was a raging bull.

I was his target.

He grabbed my collar and lifted me up off of the ground. "What do ya' think you're doin' here?! She earned that fair n' square!"

Now, I was a small fifteen year old. I admit that. But this boy seemed like a full grown man to me. He seemed nearly two feet taller than me. His hands were tough and scarred. His face showed signs of physical abuse. Greasy, dark brown hair fell over his face. He was missing a couple teeth. All he wore were two layers of dirty brown shirts, wool pants, worn out shoes, and a wool ivy cap.

"No, Scoefield! Don't hurt him!" Sarah pleaded for me. "He helped me raise this money!"

The boy looked at her, then back at me. I was still off the ground, silently panicking.

"You helped her?" He questioned me.

I nodded frantically. He set me down.

"I ain't never heard of any street boys helpin' my sister." He eyed me skeptically. "Who are ya'?"

"I'm Henry." I squeaked.

"Henry, huh?" The boy was still eyeing me. "You thinkin' about gettin' close to my sister, Henry?"

"Scoefield!" Sarah scolded.

35

"No, Mr. Scoefield." I replied quickly.

"Hey!" Scoefield yelled in my face. "You do not call me 'Mr. Scoefield', all-right?! Mr. Scoefield was my lousy pop. My name is just Scoefield."

"Yes, Scoefield." I whimpered.

"Bradley, stop it!" Sarah stepped in front of me. "He's a nice boy that just wanted to help."

"Sarah, what did I tell ya'?" Scoefield whispered angrily. "You do not call me 'Bradley' in front of bozos like this. Ya' know it's a pathetic name."

"Because of him, we made forty-three dollars today." Sarah didn't budge.

Scoefield's jaw dropped. "Forty-three? What did he do? Threaten people at gunpoint?"

"No, silly. He wrote me this." Sarah handed him my piece of paper.

I KNOW THE STRUGGLE
IN YOUR EYES, THE PAIN I SEE
HOW COULD THIS HAPPEN?
WHY WOULD GOD LET THIS BE?

FRIEND, I DON'T KNOW HOW I CAN HELP
AND I DON'T KNOW WHAT TO SAY
BUT IN MY HEART, I KNOW THIS TRUTH
THE NIGHT WILL TURN BACK TO DAY

YOU'RE NEVER TOO LOST TO BE KEPT FROM GOD
NEVER TOO HURT TO GO ON

NEVER TOO BEATEN TO TRY AGAIN
NEVER TOO FOREIGN TO BELONG

YOU'RE NEVER TOO SUNK TO BE LIFT UP
NEVER TOO FAR TO FIND YOUR HOME
NEVER TOO HOPELESS TO FIND GOD'S GRACE
AND YOU ARE NEVER ALONE

HUMAN HAND CANNOT HELP YOU
MONEY HAS ITS LIMITS
BUT IF YOU TURN TO GOD'S HOLY WORD
AND PLACE YOUR TRUST IN IT

I KNOW YOU'LL NEVER BE TOO LOST TO BE KEPT
FROM GOD
NEVER TOO HURT TO GO ON
NEVER TOO BEATEN TO TRY AGAIN
NEVER TOO FOREIGN TO BELONG

YOU'LL NEVER BE TOO SUNK TO BE LIFT UP
NEVER TOO FAR TO FIND YOUR HOME
NEVER TOO HOPELESS TO FIND GOD'S GRACE
AND YOU'LL NEVER BE ALONE

GOD HAS NOT FORGOTTEN YOU
HE WILL NOT FORSAKE YOU

LAY YOUR LIFE AT JESUS' FEET
AND THOUGH YOU'RE GOING THROUGH HARDSHIP,
HE WILL MAKE YOU NEW

STAY WITH THE MERCIFUL SAVIOUR
SUBMIT AND CARRY YOUR CROSS
YOU'LL LAY UP TREASURES YOU CAN'T IMAGINE
THAT WILL NEVER SUFFER LOSS

YOU'RE NEVER TOO LOST TO BE KEPT FROM GOD
NEVER TOO HURT TO GO ON
NEVER TOO BEATEN TO TRY AGAIN
NEVER TOO FOREIGN TO BELONG

YOU'RE NEVER TOO SUNK TO BE LIFT UP
NEVER TOO FAR TO FIND YOUR HOME
NEVER TOO HOPELESS TO FIND GOD'S GRACE
AND YOU ARE NEVER ALONE

"Churchy." Scoefield commented after reading it. "Very churchy. This worked? People gave ya' money?"
"Forty-three dollars." Sarah had a big grin on her face.
Scoefield looked back at me. "Why'd you do this for her?"
"She looked like she needed help." I told him.
"Oh, so my sister **needs** help?" Scoefield got tense again. "And you think you're the only one that can help her, huh?"
"No, sir." I shook my head.

"Hey, I ain't a 'sir' to you, either." Scoefield jabbed a finger at me.

"Bradley, stop!" Sarah slapped his hand away.

"I don't trust 'im, Sarah." Scoefield's eyes were glued on me. "People don't help for nothin'. What do ya' want, kid?"

"Nothing." I muttered.

"That's a lie!" Scoefield growled. "Everybody's always got somethin' on their minds. You tryin' to dazzle my sister? Make her go 'oo' and 'ahh' over your fancy schmancy poetry?"

"Not at all."

"Mm-hmm. Sure." Scoefield said sarcastically. "Where ya' from? What's your last name, Henry?"

I got scared. "My...last name is Engel."

"Engel? Engel?" Scoefield scratched his chin. He looked at Sarah. "I don't know any Engels. You know any Engels?" Sarah replied by shaking her head.

"Where ya' from, Engel?" Scoefield looked down at me again.

"...Nowhere." I gulped.

He grabbed my collar again. "Hey, you better tell me. If ya' were sent by them Tanner boys, you're gonna' regret it."

"I wasn't sent by anyone." I defended. "I'm...from Bonn." Scoefield let go of my collar. He turned to Sarah. Sarah shrugged.

"Bonn?" Scoefield turned back to me. "Where is that? Pennsylvania?"

"Germany." I sighed.

Both Sarah and Scoefield got surprised faces.

"You're a German?" Scoefield asked me.

I looked down at the ground. "Yes."

"You're ashamed of where ya' come from, huh?" Scoefield observed. "Hey, that's all-right with me."

I looked back up at him. A whole new face was before me. Scoefield was smiling now.

"I'm ashamed of where I come from, too." He stuck out his hand. "We haven't been properly introduced. I'm Scoefield."

I shook his hand, rather shocked at the sudden change. "...Henry Engel."

"Eh, I know who ya' are, Henry." Scoefield chuckled. "So, this churchy poem? Your mom write it?"

I was still baffled at Scoefield's reaction to my nationality. "No...I did."

"Eh, well, you'll cowboy up sooner or later." Scoefield mumbled. "So what brings ya' here instead of Germany?"

"A depression." I explained.

"Golly." Scoefield shook his head. "You got the rottenest of luck, huh?"

"No kidding." I replied.

"Your parents?"

I let out a shallow breath as I let my eyes fall to the ground. Apparently, my body language was rather clear.

Scoefield's face drooped. "Oh, you lost 'em?"

"Yes."

"You don't have anywhere to stay, do ya', Henry?"

"Well, I was at the orphanage, but-"

"The orphanage?" Scoefield scoffed. "They'll eat ya' alive if they knew you was German. Not many like Germans around here."

"Yeah, I noticed." I looked at him. "How come you do?"

"Hey, you think I'm gonna' judge someone because his country starts a war?" Scoefield shook his head again. "That was them grown-ups over there, not you.

Knuckleheads, all of 'em. Here too, sometimes. Nah, I trust a German more than I trust someone from around here."

Sarah suddenly nudged her brother. "Place to stay."

"Oh, right! You need a place to stay." Scoefield said to me. "Well, you got my sister forty-three dollars. You can stay with us."

"You have a house?" I gaped at them.

Scoefield and Sarah winced as they glanced at each other.

CHAPTER FOUR

They called them Hoovervilles, apparently. Hundreds of people living in run-down, little shacks. Scoefield and Sarah had a very simple, one room shack. It looked more like an outhouse than a shack, but I didn't want to ask if it was one. It was old and rickety, but it kept the wind out and a little bit of the cold. They had very little things: some blankets, piles of newspapers, a few buckets of water, some loaves of bread, and a worn out mattress. The shack was incredibly small. By now the orphanage was looking exceedingly better.

"Hey, don't look so disappointed." Scoefield noticed my expression. "It's better than the streets."

"Oh, yes, I agree. Thank you, Scoefield." I brightened up.

"And here, I won't get beaten up."

"Not if you behave." Scoefield laughed.

I wasn't sure if that was a joke or a threat.

Not long after we arrived, we all were settling down to sleep. Scoefield allowed me to join him and his sister on the mattress. His sister would be against the wall, Scoefield in the middle, and me on the opposite end. We used all of the blankets to cover up and slept in our day clothes. After all, none of us had any other clothes except for our day clothes. It was then that I came to realize what my new life would be like. No other clothes, no bathing (I could tell Scoefield and Sarah didn't do much of that), very limited choice on meals, no electricity, no running water, no fireplace, no space to myself…the list was growing rapidly in my head.

But then I went back to what Scoefield said.

"It's better than the streets."
I had lived on the streets of Germany. It was extremely hard, and far colder there than it was here. In reality, we shouldn't have survived. We should have died on those streets. God had blessed me with a place to stay and friends that didn't care where I came from. I left that orphanage, alone, with no place to stay, and thinking that I was going to die. Now, I had company that befriended me and kept me warm, had some money, let me stay in their home, gave me part of their mattress to sleep on…

I let *that* list grow. If one always focuses on the things that are wrong, he will never be satisfied, content, happy, or at peace. If one always focuses on the things that he is blessed with, he can be content even if he is suffering.

As Paul the Apostle wrote, while in a prison cell: "I have learned, in whatsoever state I am, *therewith* to be content". I was doing much better than a prison cell. Once again, my God was taking care of me.

I glanced over at Scoefield and Sarah. They both seemed like they were already asleep. Scoefield was cradling Sarah in his arms, as if to protect her from all dangers. As quietly as I could, I slipped out from the blankets. I got on my knees next to the mattress.

"My Lord and my God." I began to pray quietly, bowing my head. "I came to this country with my father and my mother. Now, they are with You in Your heavenly kingdom. And I am not upset at You for taking them home. You knew that they had suffered enough and it was time for their trials to be over. Please assure them that I am doing all-right. Secondly, Lord, You have blessed me far beyond I could ever deserve. You delivered me from the orphanage. You gave me a place to stay and friends to stay with. Please help me to be a blessing to them. Lord, if they do not know You, let me be a light to them. Let me be as my father was, and teach them about their sin, and Your sufferings to take the penalty of sin on Yourself. I thank You so much, Lord God. Help me to be shaped into the man You want me to be. In Jesus' name I pray, amen."

I silently moved back under the covers and soon fell asleep. The last thing I remember thinking before sleep took me was that I had prayed in English. I never before had prayed in English. I had always prayed in German. Even at the orphanage, I prayed in German. I thought it was peculiar that I prayed in English, but didn't think on it too long.

I know now that it was God that had prompted me to pray in English. How else would Sarah have understood me? After all, she had, unbeknownst to me, been awake the entire time, hearing my prayer.

"When's ya' birthday, Henry?" Scoefield asked me as we were walking down a busy street. It was 9:00 A.M. the next morning and Scoefield had told me and Sarah that we were going to have a small celebration since we had made $43 last night.

"Actually, my birthday is in ten days." I told Scoefield.

"Well, we're celebratin' it early." Scoefield grinned.

We approached a bar. I halted once I saw Scoefield and Sarah beginning to enter it.

"You comin'?" Scoefield asked me.

"I, uh, I don't want to go into a bar." I told them. "I don't think God would want me to do that."

"Seriously, kid?" Scoefield scoffed. "So, you really are churchy, aren't ya'?"

"I guess you could say that." I replied. "Proverbs says that alcohol is very foolish."

"Well, you're in luck." Scoefield said, walking over to me. "I hate beer, too. My pop was a drunk. He beat us like we were hell's children. You don't have to buy the beer, you know?"

"I know."

"So why are ya' against eating in a bar?" Scoefield pressed me.

"Because I don't want to go into Satan's territory."

"What?" Scoefield laughed. "My goodness, Henry. Wise up! Satan ain't real! That's just a scary story that parents tell so their kids will shape up. Besides, even if he was, wouldn't he be in hell, torturing people there?"

"Actually, Satan won't rule in hell, nor is he there yet." I explained. "Hell was specifically designed for him and his demons as a prison. For now, Satan walks the earth."

Scoefield looked at me like I was an idiot. "Get in the bar, boyo."

"No."

"It's cheap food."

"I'm not going."

"You want to find your own place to eat?" Scoefield threatened.

"Bradley, let's just find some place else." Sarah stepped up in between us.

Scoefield eyed her in frustration. "We've eaten at the bar for a good while now. Why are you takin' his side?"

"Because maybe we don't need to be around people that are like our father." Sarah mentioned.

Something clicked for Scoefield right then. He gave an irritated sigh.

"And we have forty-three dollars." Sarah smiled sweetly. "We can afford a little fancier this time."

Scoefield grumbled. "Just 'cause we got forty-three dollars doesn't mean we blow it all at once. Most of this is going to stuff we need. Like better clothes."

"I didn't say we had to blow it." Sarah replied. "But what's a celebration without spending just a little bit more?"

Scoefield thought on that for a second. "Actually, I got an idea of where we could go for a treat."

Freddy's Treat Shop. An ice cream place. It was in Queens. It wasn't too far from where we were. Just a decent bit of walking. Each of us were going to get an ice cream cone.

Sarah and Scoefield both got a vanilla cone. I felt like living dangerously and chose chocolate. As we enjoyed our ice cream, we began talking.

"So, Henry, tell me more about yourself." Scoefield glanced at me.

Strange to hear that. It made me think of my grandfather. First time I went fishing, my grandfather had said something similar to that.

And for the devil of it, I had no idea what to say about myself. I just sat there like a bump on a log. After the awkwardness increased, I felt I ought to say something. After all, Sarah was giving me a concerned look. Scoefield was giving me a suspicious stare.

It only made my brain work less.

"Uh-I, uh…my name is Henry." I managed.

"Gosh golly!" Scoefield's eyes bulged. "Because we must'a already forgotten that!"

"Bradley." Sarah chided gently at Scoefield's sarcasm.

"Sorry." I blushed, humiliated. "Well…I'm also German."

"What happenstance!" Scoefield continued. "We met someone *just yesterday* that *told us* that! What're the odds, Sarah?"

"Will you stop?" Sarah asked her brother.

"Let me tell ya' how this goes, Henry." Scoefield folded his hands. "We ask you to talk about yourself, and you tell us things we *don't* know."

I chuckled despite Scoefield's tone. "I apologize...um, I was born in Bonn. Bonn is in western Germany, near the border between Germany and Belgium. It's a pretty large city. It's not too much different from New York City, actually. Ludwig van Beethoven was born there, so we get some tourism."

I could tell immediately that neither Sarah nor Scoefield knew who Beethoven was. I decided I would discuss that another time.

"My father was a missionary there." I added.

Scoefield seemed confused. "Missionary?"

"Yes." I confirmed. "A man that believes God has sent him to a foreign land to preach the gospel."

"Ah, a preacher." Scoefield nodded.

"Basically." I agreed. "He met my mother there and they fell in love. They had me. I lived there for about twelve years, I suppose. Then we came here, to America. Germany isn't doing much better than here. Worse, possibly. My grandfather was taking care of us until-"

I stopped. Three years and it was still hard to talk about it.

"He died of a heart attack." I choked out. "My mother and father died a month later in a car accident."

Sarah took in a sharp, deep breath. Scoefield's face was unmoving and hard, as if he was trying to remain emotionless.

47

"That was three years ago." I finished. "I was at the orphanage ever since."

"What changed?" Sarah asked quietly.

"Another boy helped me get out." I explained. "He wanted to help me get away from all the boys that hated me. That night, I met you two."

"Wow." Scoefield commented. "That's…that's a rough story, pally. I'm really sorry. Truly."

"Me too." Sarah whispered.

"Thank you." I said.

"Why don't ya' have the funny accent?" Scoefield brought up. "Ya' sound like you were born here."

I bobbed my head around. "Well, it was best to not remind the boys in the orphanage that I was from Germany. So, I trained my voice to sound as American as possible. Now, it's a little difficult to even imagine how my German accent sounded."

Scoefield nodded, impressed. "Not bad, Henry."

"So…" I cleared my throat. "May I ask about you two?"

Before Sarah could say anything, Scoefield started muttering in a small, squeaky voice. "Uh-I, uh…my name is Scoefield."

I shook my head with a smile. He was mocking me. Sarah slapped his arm.

"Oh, you shush, Bradley Leonard!" Sarah scolded. "Shame on you!"

Scoefield ignored his sister. "Well…I'm also American."

I couldn't help but laugh. Though he was making fun of me, he had some uncanny ability for imitation. He wasn't so far off from how I actually acted.

"We've lived here our whole lives." Sarah explained to me as her brother laughed at his own clever wit. "Never left. Bradley's been around for eighteen years. Me, fifteen."

"Raised by a good Mama and a lousy Pop." Scoefield added. "Not much to tell besides that. Just been workin' to make a livin' ever since."

"Very commendable." I responded. "Working to provide for you and your sister is praiseworthy."

"Thanks, Henry." Scoefield gave a grin as he finished his ice cream cone. "So, now let's talk business."

"Business?" I raised my eyebrows.

"What business?" Sarah eyed her brother.

"The business of you stayin' at our place." Scoefield spoke in a serious tone.

"Oh." I swallowed. "I, um, don't have any money."

"No one does." Scoefield shrugged. "And I ain't lookin' for yours. But there is somethin' I will be needin' from ya'."

"Yes?" I asked, wondering what he could possibly need from me.

"Protection." Scoefield stated.

"Protection?" I was confused. I looked Scoefield up and down. He was tall, fit, and strong.

"I'm fairly certain you could wallop me, sir." I replied. Scoefield narrowed his eyes, a flicker of anger behind them. "What have I told ya' 'bout callin' me 'sir'?"

I gulped as I slunk in my seat. "Sorry, Scoefield."

"And you ain't protectin' me." He thumbed his finger at Sarah. "I want you watchin' over Sarah."

I 'ohh'ed in realization. How could I have missed it? My first encounter with Scoefield started with him worried about what I had done to Sarah. Then I became a little perplexed.

49

"But you barely know me." I answered. "How can you trust me?"

"I'm not sure if I do trust you, Henry." Scoefield replied bluntly. "But what I do know is this: if you try and hurt Sarah, you're small enough that she could beat ya' up. Of course, afterward you'll be dealin' with me. But, if you are a good guy, you'll do your best to keep her safe."

"But I'm not built for being a guardian of sorts." I reasoned. "Why me? Especially if you're not sure you can trust me."

"Because a lot of rats will attack a girl by herself. Not every skunk will attack a girl who's with someone." Scoefield informed me.

I sat back and thought on this. As I did, I noticed that my chocolate ice cream was melting.

"Look, Henry…" Scoefield spoke again, rubbing his forehead.

I focused on him. He seemed stressed.

"Let me tell ya' how it is." He looked up at me, eyes intensely fixed on me. "I work every day. Sarah is alone for five to six hours a day. Sometimes longer. Ya' saw the place we live in? A lot of desperate people. A lot of *men*."

I understood what he was saying. I nodded in comprehension.

"And I don't have many-no…" Scoefield shook his head, correcting himself. "I don't have *any* people I can trust or depend on to keep Sarah looked after while I'm gone. So, I have decided to trust you, for now. Be good to her and we'll be good to you. As long as you do that for me, you'll have a place to eat and sleep."

I was rather baffled by this. "*Eat* and sleep?"

"As long as ya' help." Scoefield nodded. "It won't be too fillin', but it'll keep ya' alive."

I took a moment to breathe that all in. I was to be a protector. Watch this young girl known as Sarah Scoefield. And the payment for this was a roof over my head, food in my belly, and a mattress to sleep on. And no judgment for who I was. These Americans were showing great kindness to a German like me. I could now see God's plan for getting me out of the orphanage.

I couldn't help but start to tear up. "God has been so good to me through you two."

Scoefield creased his eyebrows in puzzlement. Sarah just blinked.

I bowed my head. "*Danke.* Thank you, I mean. Thank you so much."

There was a long pause, but eventually I heard Scoefield softly say:

"You're welcome."

As noted earlier, my job was simple: make sure Sarah stayed safe and content. For the next couple weeks, I did exactly that. It was strange because I basically just followed her around wherever she decided to go. Whether she was going to sing on a street corner, go window-shopping, or just take a walk. All the while, I was able to get to know Sarah better and better.

Scoefield, after putting a little bit of the money away for emergencies, bought Sarah and even me some new clothing. I was given a thick brown shirt, some old overalls, and some long-johns. Scoefield simply got himself some new shoes. He seemed to be satisfied with the clothing he had at the time. Sarah was the one who was given the worthy portion of the money that was spent. A new, yellow polka-dot blouse, a dark green skirt that nearly touched her ankles, and a thick, warm, red coat. Scoefield wanted to make sure she wasn't cold anymore when walking about. I was grateful enough just to have gotten some new clothes. The overalls were new to me, but I was able to manage.

A month passed as I played defender of the innocent, and it had come to my attention that I was starting to stay away from church. In my daily Bible reading, I came across Hebrews 10:25 – "Not forsaking the assembling of ourselves together, as the manner of some *is;*"
It was weighing on me. I knew I was supposed to be in church.
"I'm supposed to look after you every day, correct?" I asked Sarah as we were on our way to a place she simply called 'the diner'. She told me that it was where Scoefield worked and she wanted to pay him a visit.
"Yes." Sarah responded as we continued down the sidewalk.
"What about Sundays?"
"Well, since Sunday is a day, I suppose it belongs in the category of 'every day', don't you think?" Sarah giggled.
I sighed. "I guess so."
Sarah eyed me, her smile lessening. "Why? What's wrong?"
"I miss church."
"You *like* church?" Sarah seemed surprised.
I replied, a little surprised myself. "You don't?"
"All you do is sit there, listening to a guy talk for a couple of hours." Sarah said. "How can anyone like it?"
I took that into account. "I see…I reckon that it's not exactly about *liking* church as it is *needing* church."

"Needing church?" Sarah asked.

"Yes." I nodded. "I most certainly need church."

"Why? Your parents?"

I nodded again. However, that wasn't the whole reason. "That's part of it." I explained. "My grief is comforted by God and by others there at the church. But that's not all. Going to church is about learning how to live the way God would want you to live."

"Bradley hates church." Sarah mentioned, somewhat randomly. "I don't remember what it was like. We went when we were real little kids, but he never wants to go back."

"That's sad, if you ask me." I scratched the back of my neck.

"If you want to go…" Sarah said hesitantly. "But you still want to keep the deal with Bradley about watching me… maybe I could go with you."

"You want to?" I pondered. Just a moment ago, she seemed to make it clear that she didn't think highly of church. Sarah gazed at me, right in the eyes. "If that's what you want, Henry."

Before I could say anything more, Sarah turned back around and faced a small, beaten down building. "Here we are."

I looked it up and down without saying anything. I knew times were bad, so I needed not criticize. The windows were all cracked or not there at all. Where a window was missing, wood was boarded up where the glass should have been. The building was made of brick, but it didn't look very stable. The door appeared as if it would fall off its hinges at any moment. The name of the diner above the door was so faded out that it couldn't be read. I guess that's why we always just called it 'the diner'. Sarah and I entered the diner. It wasn't doing so well on the inside either, by the look of it. The lights needed replaced, the walls weren't the cleanest, chairs were rickety if not broken, tables were old and worn. Many dark-skinned people were sitting, enjoying their meals. It wasn't the first time I had seen people that had dark brown skin, but it was still new to me.

I suppose I stared a little. Some people were glaring back at me, as if I had said something offensive.

"Well, hi, honey." A dark-skinned woman approached Sarah and I. She wore a simple, blue collared dress with a white apron around her waist. She had a pen and pad of paper in hand.

"Hi, Nancy." Sarah smiled brightly. "Mind if we get a bite to eat?"

"Oh, darlin', you're always welcome here." Nancy gave a bright, genuine smile.

She noticed me. "Now who might this be?"

"I'm Henry." I said timidly.

Nancy gave Sarah a very peculiar look as she hummed "Mm-hmmmm."

Sarah blushed.

"How about I get you two seated?" Nancy gave a laugh.

"Thanks Nancy." Sarah squeaked, still blushing.

Nancy led us to an unsteady table next to the window. "Here are a couple of menus." Nancy handed them to us. "I'll be right back."

She quickly zipped off to help someone else.

"She's nice." I spoke up to Sarah.

"Yeah." Sarah was avoiding eye-contact with me.

"Are you okay?"

Sarah bit her lip. "Yeah. Fine."

"So, Scoefield works here?" I asked.

Sarah seemed relieved at the change of subject. "Oh yes. He's the cook."

I raised my eyebrows. "Scoefield can cook?"

"We both can." Sarah replied. "He learned first, though. He had to after our parents died."

"I see." I nodded. "So do they let you eat cheap here?"

"The diner is relatively cheap already." Sarah explained. "Negro diners aren't very expensive."

I stopped for a moment. "What did you call this place?"

Sarah blinked at me. "A Negro diner."

"What's a Negro diner?"

Sarah gestured around. "You haven't noticed the Negro people around us?"

I actually had noticed, but didn't assume that it was only for dark-skinned people.

"Why are they called 'Negro'?" I brought up instead.

"That's what they want to be called." Sarah informed me. "There are other...worse names for them. But Scoefield and I never say them. It's mean. They like being called 'Negro', so that's what we say."

"Oh." Was all I said.

After a moment of silence, Sarah and I simultaneously looked at our menus.

"What are you thinking of having?" I questioned Sarah as I glanced over the options.

"I'm trying to decide if I want to try something new or something I already love." Sarah replied.

"Does Scoefield cook a mean burger?"

She laid down her menu and smiled at me. "Why don't you find out?"

At that moment, Nancy reappeared at our table.

"You two ready?"

"Yes, ma'am." I set my menu down. "Oh, I mean, if you are, Sarah."

"I am." She smiled.

"All-right." Nancy took out her pen and pad of paper. "What'll it be?"

"You first." I gestured toward Sarah.

She giggled before answering. "I'll have the pork tenderloin and a cola."

"Mm-hmmm." Nancy hummed as she scribbled away with her pen. "And you, young man?"

"I'll take a burger. And a lemon lime soda, please."

"All-right." Nancy gave a bright smile again. "I'll take those menus off your hands and be back in a jiffy."

She hurried off to the back. Sarah and I were about to begin more conversation when…

"She's here?" Scoefield's unmistakable voice echoed from the back. "Nancy! You gotta' tell me these things!"

Suddenly, he burst through the door. I tried to hold back my laughter. He was dressed in a large apron and had a hair net over his head. He looked rather ridiculous.

"Sarah!" Scoefield gleamed. "What'cha doin', visitin' your brother on a day like this? C'mere you!"

Sarah leaped up and gave her brother a big hug. Then she stepped back.

"Oh, you're all greasy!"

"Well, of course I am! I'm makin' a pork tenderloin and a burger for you two." He gave us both a wink. "Hey! Henry, you keep an eye on her. She's known to get into trouble."

I laughed. "I will, Scoefield."

56

"You better." Scoefield laughed back. "Now, if you'll excuse me, I got work to do."

He rushed back into the kitchen. Sarah sat down, getting some napkins to wipe off the grease that was now on her. I noticed there was some on her cheek.

"You got some right here." I gestured to my own cheek to show her where.

She missed it.

"No, the other side." I chuckled.

She missed it again.

I sighed with a smile. I grabbed a napkin. "Here."

I reached across the table and wiped her face. She immediately drew in a breath as I did this and gave me a very serious look.

"Are you okay?" I asked as I sat back down.

She blushed again. "Yeah. I'm fine."

Just then, Nancy was walking over with our sodas. She set them down on our table.

"One cola, and one lemon lime." She said happily.

At that moment, something else caught my attention. Outside the window, three obnoxiously loud boys were parading down the sidewalk. They were guffawing and pointing into the diner.

Then they barged in.

"Well, howdy y'all!" One of the boys yelled out in the diner.

I was confused. What on earth were they doing? Sarah seemed instantly infuriated, as did most of the other customers. Nancy seemed worried.

"Hey, coloured lady!" One of the boys jeered at Nancy. "How about getting one of your best coloured steaks in here?"

"Probably almost as good as the worst thing you've ever tasted!" One of the other boys laughed.

Then they all broke out into hideous laughter.

"You boys need to leave if you're going to be like that." Nancy put her hands on her hips. "There's no need to disturb anyone here."

Upon hearing this, the boys' entire mood changed. Anger.

The leader of them tromped up to Nancy, looking like he was ready to beat her down. Nancy began to step back, while fear filled her eyes.

"What did you say to us?" Then he said something that Sarah said I should not repeat. It was a vile word.

Nancy was slightly shaking as everyone else in the room was silent. "I said...you need to leave."

"No cow like you is going to tell me what to do!" The boy yelled at her. Then he raised his fist.

"HEY!" Scoefield burst through the back door. He saw what was happening and without a moment of hesitation, grabbed the boy's arm and twisted it backwards. The boy cried out like a whimpering dog. Scoefield then threw him into an empty table, knocking it over.

"What'cha think you're doin' here, Tanner boys?!" Scoefield raged. "Get out!"

"You don't own us, Scoefield!" The oldest Tanner boy got up off the ground. "My daddy will make you pay!"

"You're daddy couldn't make me pay even if he was selling me something!" Scoefield shot back.

"So, what, Scoefield?" One of the other Tanner boys spoke up. "You a Negro lover?"

Scoefield's rage was building, I could see it. He snapped his head to look at the other boys.

"Actually, I'm a people lover. You boys should try it sometime."

"They ain't people!" The youngest Tanner boy responded. "They're nothing but freed slaves! My grand-pappy said so!"

That did it. Scoefield broke. He flew at them, hitting them with so many punches that you couldn't see his fists. The oldest Tanner boy ran to help his brothers, but was only elbowed in the face and then slammed onto the ground. All by Scoefield.

After he had knocked the fire out of all of them, he picked up the two younger ones by their collars. He placed his foot on the oldest one's head.

"Now you boys listen *real* careful." Scoefield's voice was quiet and sparking with anger. "You are in the presence of some fine men and women. Gentlemen and ladies. And you better treat them like gentlemen and ladies before I treat *you* like slaves. Now apologize to 'em!"

"Sorry! Sorry!" All of them yelped.

"Good." Scoefield gritted his teeth. "Now GET OUT!"

He nearly threw the two younger boys out the door. He kicked the oldest.

"You should know better than to mess with my diner, Tom." Scoefield growled as the oldest scrambled out the door.

Nancy gave a huge sigh of relief. "Thank you, Scoefield."

"Anytime, ma'am." Scoefield replied politely. "Them boys need to learn respect."

And Scoefield walked back into the kitchen.

It took a little while, but everything went back to normal. There were many things that I did not understand.

59

"Why did they do that?" I whispered to Sarah. "Why were they acting like..."

"Brutes?" Sarah finished my question. "Because that's what they are."

"They do that to *everybody*?" I was astounded.

"Everybody they can pick on." Sarah nodded. "Mostly Negroes, though."

"Why?"

"Because they think they're better than them." Sarah said it like it was obvious. "A lot of people are like that. Being white is being superior in the minds of most men."

A shadowy chill fell over me. I had heard people in Germany beginning to speak of "being superior" before I left.

"That's terrible." I sighed.

"Yeah."

"So, Scoefield knows those boys?"

Sarah nodded. "He's not fond of them, by any means. Tom, Randy, and Charlie Tanner. They like to mess around with anyone they can. They use to mess with me, when I would sing on the sidewalk. Then I told Bradley about them."

"He roughed them up?" I asked.

Sarah's eyes widened as she shook her head. "He put Tom in the hospital. Bradley could have gotten in so much trouble for that, but Tom never ratted on him because he was scared of what Bradley would've done if he did say anything."

"Not too bright, are they?" I let out a small laugh.

"Not the sharpest tools in the shed." Sarah agreed.

Around that time, Nancy brought out our food.

"Thanks, Nancy." Sarah smiled.

"Yes, thank you, ma'am." I smiled as well.

"It is my pleasure." Nancy said happily.

As she left, I took my first bite. "Wow, this is good."

"I'm glad you think so." Sarah giggled.

"That was fast service!" I told her with a mouth full of food.

"Bradley may have put our orders first when they came in." Sarah mentioned as she took tiny bites of her tenderloin. "He tends to do that when I eat here."

"That's nice of him." I said, finally able to get the large bite down.

"Hey...Henry?" Sarah asked quietly as I got halfway done with my burger.

"Hmm?" Was all I could say, my mouth was full again.

"Can I ask you something personal?"

"Sure."

"How did your parents die? In the car accident. What happened?"

I set my burger down. "A...A truck driver ran a stop sign and hit us."

"I am very sorry." Sarah sympathized.

"Thank you."

"My parents died in a car accident too." Sarah spoke solemnly.

I raised my eyebrows at that. Yes, I knew that Sarah and Scoefield were orphans, but I didn't expect for her to actually tell me about it though.

"Really?" Was all I could think to say.

"Mm-hmm." Sarah replied. "Our father...he was a drunk. He got drunk a lot of times. He would beat our mom. Sometimes, Bradley would stand up to him. Try and keep him away from Mama and me. Sometimes that worked....sometimes that didn't. One day, Bradley told me that he was going to go with Mama and Pop to the candy store and he would pick up something for me."

Sarah closed her eyes. "I think he was trying to protect me, because Mama would never want me left alone in the house. But I think Pop was drunk. When he was drunk, if you didn't do what he said, he would beat you. So, they drove off and I stayed at home. A couple hours later, Bradley came home. His arm was bleeding. Pop had been drunk and…"

She stopped to wipe some tears away.

"He and Mama were at the bottom of a river, still in the car."

I let out a shocked breath. I had seen drunkards before, but I had never heard their children speak.

"Sarah…I…I am very sorry."

It was exactly what she had said to me, and I know it didn't do much. But I still wanted to say something.

"Thank you." She wiped her eyes again.

CHAPTER FIVE

After finishing our meal, generously tipping Nancy, and saying goodbye to Scoefield, we began to head home. I felt touched that Sarah had shared the story of her parents with me. It was not an everyday thing for someone to confide so much into a person that she didn't know all that well.

I felt like she trusted me. And if I was going to be honest, I trusted her.

We chatted about little things on our walk home. We talked about our favorite seasons, the differences between Germany and America, why Sarah's hair was such a fuss to her, the list went on and on.

I was happy. It was nice to have such a good friend. And the blessings kept on coming. On our way back to the shack, I spotted something shining in the snow. It was two dimes and two nickels. I offered to give them to Sarah, but she refused, saying that they were my money. I eventually put them in my pocket as we continued our hopeless, happy conversations. It was dumb of me, however.

I didn't realize that we were being followed. It was getting dark, too. We plodded past a street that was rather empty of people. That's when I was shoved down into the snow and Sarah was grabbed.

The Tanner boys.

"There you are, little miss princess!" Tom grabbed Sarah as Randy and Charlie surrounded her.

"Let go of me, Tom!" Sarah spat. "Scoefield will have your hide when he finds this out!"

Tom began pulling her hair, making her cry. "Scoefield ain't going to find out about this! If he does, little lover-boy Benny gets the beating of his life!"

"His name is Henry, you scumbag!"

"Whatever!" Tom pulled her hair again.

I couldn't believe my eyes when I saw it. These boys had just taken a mighty beating from Sarah's older brother and now, they were targeting her. I quickly pushed myself out of the snow. This time, there was no Scoefield to save Sarah.

It was up to me. It was up to me.

This was my job.

This was why Scoefield had me around Sarah. And I cared for Sarah. I couldn't let them hurt her. I needed to do something. I mustered up my courage.

"Hey!" I tried my best to sound like Scoefield. Four sets of eyes all turned to me. The little German boy. I was nearly smaller than Charlie, who was only thirteen at the time.

"Oh, little Benny is going to be brave, huh?" Tom taunted as he threw Sarah to Randy. Randy pulled on her hair violently.

Tom made a taunting gesture at me. "Come on, punk. Show us what'cha got."

I swelled my chest. I was angry. But what could I really do about it?

I tried a bluff. I shouted the biggest threat I could in German. In English, it basically means 'Shut your mouth and get lost!'.

All three boys seemed baffled. I was hoping it would intimidate them.

I was wrong.

"A German?!" Tom raved. He charged at me and swung a hammer-like fist at me. Fortunately, I was smart enough to duck. Tom missed and almost made himself fall on the pavement. I took my chance as Tom was regaining his footing. I balled up my fist. I reeled it back. I flung it forward with all of my strength, right into Tom's ribcage. I'm fairly certain a baby rabbit could do better than I did that day. I merely hit what felt like bricks, cradled my hurt hand and then received one of the hardest punches I had ever experienced in my life. I was down and I was seeing stars. Luckily, the real fighter came.

"What do I have to do to get it through you boys' heads?!" I could hear Scoefield roar.
As it turns out, Scoefield had been let off of work early and came running after us.
God was yet again looking after me.
I opened my eyes to see Scoefield fly in like a lion. Ferocious, wild, and spitting-mad, Scoefield knocked Tom down with a punch that was twice as hard as stone. I could hear Tom's teeth crunch from the force of it. Picking Tom up, Scoefield tossed him like a rag-doll into Charlie. Randy had let go of Sarah, running for the hills, but was stopped short when Scoefield kicked him down. Scoefield dragged them all together and began walloping them. With fists as hard as iron and fast as whips. Pummeling them like they were as evil as demons.
But Scoefield was the one that was as scary as one.
I watched, absolutely shocked by what was before me. His eyes blazed like a predator. His teeth grit and he bared them viciously. And the blows only struck harder and harder.
Scoefield was not easing up on them. If anything, he was increasing in ferocity.
"*Is he going to kill them?*" I gasped.

"Scoefield!" I called. "That's enough!"

"Bradley!" Sarah ran to him and began pulling at Scoefield's shirt. "Stop, Bradley!"

Scoefield suddenly came out of his rampage. His hands had blood on them. The boys were cringing in both pain and fear. Even Tom, who was around Scoefield's age. Charlie was crying.

"Please…we're sorry." Tom muttered with blood flowing from his nose. It seems he had also lost a tooth.

For a moment, Scoefield looked horrified himself. That he could be capable of such monstrous brutality. Then, his anger regained control.

"You touch my sister again, and you'll regret it." Scoefield growled low. "And don't ya' even think about tellin' anyone. Or I'll pound ya' harder."

One by one, they swore not to. Then Scoefield kicked Tom in the side while he shouted at them to leave.

They did so. I watched them as they quickly made their way away from us, trying not to get blood on their clothes.

"Are you all-right, Henry?" Scoefield approached me, holding out his hand to help me up. I hesitated and simply looked at him for a second. This man I knew…I had never seen such anger and malicious intent before in anyone.

I was frightened, deeply frightened of him. And he could see it, I knew. He saw the same look in my eyes as he saw in Tom's, Randy's, and Charlie's.

Shame overtook his countenance as he pulled back his hand. "I-…I'm sorry you had to see that…I…I just meant to rough them up a bit."

I stood up to my feet. I tried to lift his spirits. "Thank you for helping us. They would have thrashed us had you not come."

Scoefield smiled at that, but I could still see the regret in his eyes.

"Let's go home." I smiled.

"I know I must seem like a monster to ya', Henry." Scoefield spoke.

It was late and Sarah was in bed, fast asleep. Scoefield asked me if he could talk with me outside. I suppose the fight was hanging heavy over his head.

"You were angry." I replied. "I understand."

"I wasn't angry, I was fumin' with rage." Scoefield kicked a rock. "I was actin' like a mad bull. I was actin'..." Scoefield closed his eyes, a disgusted look on his face. "...I was actin' like my pop. I was actin' just like Amos Scoefield."

"You are not your father, Scoefield." I reassured him. "His decisions are not your destiny."

"Where'd you get that?" Scoefield half-chuckled. "Candy wrapper?"

"I got it from the Bible." I answered.

Scoefield muttered at that. I wasn't sure what else to say to him. I put my hands in my pockets, suddenly feeling the thirty cents I had picked up earlier. An idea popped into my head.

"You want a soda pop?" I asked Scoefield.

He narrowed his eyes at me. "Like we should use our money to spend on soda pop."

"I found thirty cents."

"You did?"

I nodded.

Scoefield's face softened. He thought on it. "What about Sarah?"

"We won't be gone long." I promised him. "And we can bring her one back. What does she like?"

"Cola." Scoefield told me. He thought on it some more. He opened the door to the house and peeked in. Sarah was still fast asleep.

"All-right." Scoefield whispered. "But let's make it quick."

We began heading down the road. I had remembered that my father had told me, when we were in Germany, that some people would not come to God because they got the Bible shoved in their face night and day. He said that sometimes people came to God because of seeing His nature in believers. In showing Scoefield kindness, friendship, and generosity, I had hoped I could get him to open up towards God through those means. And, in order to allow Scoefield to become more comfortable with the situation thus far, I decided to stop talking about God for a while.

"Which flavor will you get?" I questioned Scoefield.

Scoefield pondered. "Root beer. Love that stuff. Haven't had one for a year now."

"A year?" I marveled. "They are only ten cents."

"I've been needin' every penny I can get." Scoefield explained. "In fact, we should be savin' the thirty cents you found…"

"There won't be any harm in getting a few sodas." I smiled. "Trust me."

Scoefield mumbled but said nothing.

We walked a little further without saying anything until…

"Have you even had a soda pop before?" Scoefield gave me a questioning look.

"Twice." I told him. "Once today and once with my grandfather. I had lemon-lime soda both times. It was so bubbly and exhilarating."

Scoefield laughed. "You're a strange one."

"So I have been told." I agreed with a smile.

We found a malt shop that wasn't too far away from home. Scoefield got himself a root beer and Sarah a cola. I, of course, bought a lemon-lime. As soon as we paid for them, we began heading back to make sure Sarah wasn't left by herself for too long.

"How can I help?" I started the conversation.

Scoefield raised an eyebrow as he took a gulp from his root beer. "Help?"

"Help out with anything. Money-wise or other." I clarified.

Scoefield shrugged. "Not many jobs around, so ya' probably can't with money."

"But I want to be a blessing, Scoefield." I urged him. "I'll find a job, if you need me to."

Scoefield responded by shaking his head with a smile.

"You're a strange one, Henry. Don't ya' get it? You *are* helpin' me. You have a job. Your job is Sarah. As long as you do that, you're helpin' tons. Besides, there's no jobs to go around. You sure ain't gettin' my job."

"Thank you, Scoefield." I smiled, feeling better.

"Eh, don't mention it, Henry." Scoefield shrugged as we continued down the cold sidewalk.

Before he could say anything else, I hugged him. It was quick, but Scoefield still shoved me.

"Hey, enough of that." He eyed me. "I don't do hugs, Henry."

"Not even your friends?" I opened my arms again, inviting him for a hug.

69

"Who says you're my friend?" He raised an eyebrow at me.

"Since when does Scoefield get a job for someone who isn't his friend?" I grinned.

Scoefield narrowed his eyes at me. Suddenly, he let out a small laugh.

"Come on." I egged him on. "Give your buddy a hug."

"You lousy kid." Scoefield grinned.

And he gave me a hug. After about two seconds, however, he wrapped one arm around my head while taking his free hand and rubbing his knuckles into my crown.

I was later told that it was called a "noogie". It seemed like something a big brother would do to a little brother, which I suppose made me feel good. In essence, Scoefield was treating me like family.

"You are a lousy kid." Scoefield laughed again and released me.

"Now look what you've done." I chuckled. "You messed up my hair."

"You mean that mop on your head?" Scoefield began walking ahead of me as it began to lightly sleet. "You need a haircut, Henry."

"So do you, Scoefield." I smirked. "I don't even know how you can see through that."

"Eh, I just push it outta' the way." Scoefield shrugged. "Mine listens to me, but yours is wild and does what it wants. You need a haircut more than me."

"I'll get right on that." I joked as I followed behind. "As soon as you buy me some scissors."

"Oh, and should I get you a candy bar with it?" Scoefield turned around and mockingly bowed to me. "Your Baroness?"

70

I couldn't help but guffaw. "You just called me a female noble!"

"What? Well, whatever you guys call it over there!" Scoefield chortled back. "Doesn't matter! You're in America now! You talk like we do!"

"I talk more like an American than you do!" I pointed at him, still laughing.

"Hey!" Scoefield was pretending to be angry. "Them's fightin' words, pally."

"See?" I was dying with laughter.

We continued to joke and mess around like that most of the walk home. After a while, we calmed down and simply slung our arm around each other as we walked. Every now and again, we would sip our drinks.

"Scoefield?" I asked as the light mush began to soak through my shirt.

"Hm?"

"Thank you."

"Hey, I already told ya'." Scoefield nudged me. "Don't mention it."

"No, not about all you've done for me." I explained. "Thank you for being my best friend. God knew I needed one here."

Scoefield looked at me for a moment in silence as we kept walking. "Best friend, eh? My, you've picked a cruddy one."

"I don't think so." I spoke genuinely.

Scoefield glanced at me again. He tried to hide it, but I could tell he was touched. "You really believe God is always lookin' out for ya'?"

"Yes." I told him. "Have you ever read the book of Esther?"

71

"Nah."

"Well, did you know that God isn't mentioned once in it?"

"No kiddin'?" Scoefield was surprised. "And that's in the Bible? They leave God out of His own Bible?"

I smiled. "In Esther, they do. God's name doesn't appear one single time. There are no miracles done, no prophecies, nothing supernatural. Yet, it is one of the greatest writings on the providence of God."

"Stop using big words with me, boyo." Scoefield replied. "I got no idea what proclamence is."

"*Providence*..." I emphasized with a small chuckle. "Is like providing. God provided for His children. Much like you are providing for Sarah."

"Okay, I get the picture." Scoefield nodded in comprehension.

"Well, this Jewish girl, Esther, she's in a foreign land: Persia. And her people are in danger. A man is trying to kill them all off. Complete and total Jewish genocide. However, before this ever comes to light, Esther is made queen of Persia. She-"

"Whoa, Henry!" Scoefield interrupted me. "Back up! She's a normal girl and then 'pow' she's queen?"

"It is a long story." I nodded. "A lot does happen...Hey, Scoefield? How about I just read it to you? That way, you'll get the whole picture."

Scoefield took a deep breath. "Read the Bible to me? I don't know, Henry. It's a bore and it uses words I can't understand."

"Just give it a chance." I pleaded. "Sarah can be there too."

Scoefield thought about it. "Eh. How bad could it be?"

"*Thank you, God.*" I prayed. Scoefield was opening his heart to God's Word.

CHAPTER SIX

I opened up the Bible to Esther. Sarah and Scoefield both waited, sitting on the mattress. This was actually two months later. In spring, as a matter of fact. Scoefield had a tendency of shrugging off our Bible reading.

One night, it was "Too tired".

Another night, it was "Not in the mood".

Most nights, he simply said "Nah".

Although he had told me that one night that we would go through the Bible, it was difficult to get him to keep his word.

But in April, I received some support.

Scoefield walked in the door after a long day at work. I opened my mouth, ready to ask the same question I had continually asked for two months.

"Don't even ask." Scoefield stopped me before I could even utter the first syllable.

I closed my mouth, certain that was the end of the conversation. But I was wrong.

"You told him you would." Sarah spoke up.

"Excuse me?" Scoefield turned to Sarah.

"You, Bradley Leonard, told Henry you would read the Bible with him." Sarah gave Scoefield a cross glare.

"Oh, you must'a been hidin' in the bushes." Scoefield retaliated. "Because I don't recall you bein' there for that conversation."

"You *told* me that you said you would do it." Sarah fired back.

"Well, I lied." Scoefield folded his arms. "Because I actually said 'How bad could it be?'."

"That's no different."

"Yes, it is."

"How?" Sarah narrowed her eyes.

"I didn't say I would." Scoefield defended. "I just said that it-actually, no! I asked a question! Ha! I didn't promise nothin'!"

Scoefield smirked triumphantly as he turned to the water buckets.

"Bradley." Sarah said in a dangerously low voice.

"What?" Scoefield asked as he splashed some water on his face.

"You implied that you would." Sarah reasoned. "'How bad could it be?' is equivalent to saying 'yes' in our common terminology. You back out now, you're not a man of your word."

Scoefield slowly pivoted to look Sarah in the eye. His face had utter amazement and confusion on it. "Where in the blazes did you learn that smart talk?"

Sarah blushed and smiled simultaneously. I, on the other hand, quickly lowered my head, acting as if something had taken my attention. Eventually, something did. A bug was crawling across the floor. A little wood louse. I found them cute. A wood louse could also be known as a 'roly poly'. I was pleasantly distracted by the adorable creature. I felt Scoefield's eyes on me, though. I continued staring at my roly poly. Thankfully, Sarah saved me.

"Just give it a try, Bradley." Sarah urged.

Scoefield gave a deep sigh. "Fine."

So, moments later, my Bible was open. Sarah seemed curious and even eager to hear from the Bible. Scoefield seemed more like he was about to hear me read from the dictionary.

I paused. "There's a little bit of background information I have to give you."

"Why are we starting in the middle of the book?" Sarah asked.

"Scoefield said-" I was about to say.

"We aint goin' to understand it if you start in the middle, Henry." Scoefield interrupted. "Start from the beginnin'."

"Very well." I began to flip to Genesis. I cleared my throat. "In the beginning God created the heaven and the earth. And the earth was without form, and void; and darkness *was* upon the face of the deep. And the Spirit of God moved upon the face of the waters. And God said, Let there be light: and there was light. And God saw the light, that *it was* good: and God divided the light from the darkness. And God called the light Day, and the darkness he called Night. And the evening and the morning were the-"

I stopped, looking up at Sarah and Scoefield.

Both were deeply perplexed.

"Henry?"

"Yes, Sarah?"

"What does 'void' mean?"

"Well, it means…um empty, I guess." I scratched my head.

"It starts rather…fast." Scoefield squinted. "Didn't ya' say there was background stuff?"

"Well, I-"

"Can't you just tell us without all the fancy schmancy?" Scoefield questioned.

I hesitated for a moment. I set my Bible on the mattress. "Okay."

I took a moment to collect my thoughts. "God…has always been. He has never had a birth like we would know.

There was never a time when He did not exist. He has always been."

I let that sink in for a moment.

"That's impossible." Scoefield stated. "Everyone has a beginnin'. Every*thing* has a beginnin'."

"Not God." I shook my head. "And honestly, I can't comprehend it. I don't know how to explain it or how to understand it. I just have to accept it as truth."

Scoefield scoffed but said nothing more.

"So…" I continued. "Some time in the expanse of eternity past, God created everything we know: the earth, the sky, the animals, the oceans, us, everything. He created a man named Adam. And God put Adam in the Garden of Eden, instructing Adam to take care of the garden and to name all of the animals."

"Adam named all of the animals?" Sarah asked. "*All* of them?"

I nodded.

"Even flies?"

I nodded with a smile.

"That seems dumb." Scoefield muttered. "Of all the things that can fly, this Adam guy gave the name 'fly' to a bug? Why not to a bird? Why not name birds 'fly'?"

Sarah and I both laughed at that.

"Well, that's a good question." I laughed. "I don't know, Adam just did it the way he thought it should be."

"That means he also named donkeys 'donkey'." Sarah giggled.

"Poor animals." Scoefield snickered back. "They didn't even have a chance."

"Anyway, those were Adam's first jobs." I got back on track. "Naming the animals and taking care of the Garden of Eden. But God felt that Adam was...lonely."

I glanced at Sarah.

"So, God gave him a woman."

Scoefield whistled. "Now yer' talkin!"

"Bradley, let him finish." Sarah scolded.

"God put Adam in a deep sleep one day." I explained. "And God took one of Adam's ribs, and from it, formed woman."

Sarah's mouth dropped. "I'm a rib?"

Scoefield burst out laughing, pointing at his sister mockingly.

"Don't laugh." I told Scoefield with a smile. "You and I are dirt."

Scoefield stopped. "Wait, what?"

"God formed man out of the dust of the ground." I told him.

Sarah laughed back at Scoefield.

"And on that day, God preformed the first marriage." I said to them. "Adam and the woman, who was called Eve. The first husband and wife."

Sarah let out an 'aww' while Scoefield rolled his eyes.

"And for that moment in time, Adam and Eve lived in perfect harmony with each other and with all of creation." I said.

"That can't be true." Scoefield shook his head skeptically. "You're tellin' me that they didn't have one fight? One argument? This sounds like a fairy-tale."

"Well, Scoefield, they *were* perfect because sin had not yet been introduced to mankind."

"Sin?"

"Yes, sin." I explained. "It's all the bad things we do. Sin is in all of us today. It's why we lie, why we want other people's things, why we get angry, why we have arguments, why we have wars, why we have bullies, and racism, and hatred, and guilt, and judgment, and sorrow."

Scoefield gave me a look of anger. "Then why would God let sin happen to us?"

I took a breath. "Scoefield, do you love Sarah?"

"Of course."

"Do you want her to love you?" I asked.

"She *does* love me." Scoefield growled.

"Yes, I know, but I what I mean is…" I paused to collect the right words. "Okay, imagine Sarah falls in love with a guy."

Sarah began to blush.

"And he wants to take Sarah to a far away place. Away from you, Scoefield. If she wanted to go with him, would you force her to stay with you?"

Scoefield seemed confused at my question. "Is he a good man? Will he take care of her?"

I shook my head. "Okay, bad example. Umm…okay, imagine that Sarah wanted to just leave you. She wanted to leave far away. And she would never see you ever again. Would you force her to stay even though she wanted to leave?"

Scoefield understood this time. "…No. I wouldn't."

"Why not?"

"Because…I won't make her do somethin' she doesn't want to do." Scoefield replied.

"The same is true with God." I told him. "If God forced us to love Him and always do what He wanted, it wouldn't really be love. We would be more like tools or toys. Just there whenever God wanted us to do whatever He wanted. So, God gave us a choice."

"A choice to do what?" Sarah asked.

"To choose Him or choose ourselves." I said sadly. "God planted a certain tree in the Garden of Eden. The tree of the knowledge of good and evil. God told Adam to never eat of the fruit of that tree. If Adam ate of the fruit, God told him he would die."

"And he ate it, didn't he?" Scoefield concluded.

"Eventually." I responded. "And sin entered the hearts of humanity."

Scoefield stood up in anger. "So it's because of that rat that we got to live like this?!"

"Calm down." I told Scoefield. "He didn't do it by himself. See, Satan was the first creature to have sin. He was an angel, but was corrupted with pride. He hated God and he hated Adam and Eve. So, he disguised himself as a snake and approached Eve in the garden. He asked her if she was allowed to eat of the tree of the knowledge of good and evil. Eve said no, because they would die if they did. But Satan lied to her and said they wouldn't die. They would, instead, gain knowledge and be like little gods. So Eve ate the fruit."

Sarah slumped. "The woman sinned first?"

"Makes sense." Scoefield coughed under his breath.

"I heard that." Sarah eyed him.

"She was deceived." I stated. "She bought the lie. Adam, however, was never tricked. He found Eve and that she had eaten the forbidden fruit. Eve thought he should eat of it, too. And Adam, knowing it was wrong, ate it."

"He chose love." Sarah gave a small smile.

79

I frowned. "You may be right, but the consequence of his disobedience to God was devastating. This was not an honorable act. It was rebellion. And they knew they had done wrong immediately. They felt guilty. Up to this point, Adam and Eve had never felt guilt because they had never done anything wrong. And when they heard God walking in the garden, they hid themselves from Him. God knew what they had done and He had to punish them for their sin."

"But I don't understand." Sarah blurted out. "It was just a fruit. Why would God be so mean?"
"God is not mean." I replied. "He is holy. And holiness cannot be in the presence of sin. Sin must be punished. Like when a crime is committed. Say someone murders a family. He has to receive judgment because he has done something terrible."
"But I still don't understand." Sarah said again. "It was just some fruit."
I sighed. "To be honest, Sarah, I think the same thing sometimes. It doesn't seem that big of a deal, but the fact remains that God told them to stay away from something and they did not. It's…like how parents tell their kids not to play in the streets. In reality, playing in the street is not that bad of a thing. But if a car comes around, the child could be hit and die. It is similar to that, I suppose."
Sarah seemed to understand.

I continued. "God punished all three of them: Adam, Eve, and Satan. Adam's punishment was to, from then on, have to work hard. He had to work before, but it was never hard work. The Bible says that God said: 'cursed *is* the ground for thy sake; in sorrow shalt thou eat *of* it all the

days of thy life; Thorns also and thistles shall it bring forth
to thee; and thou shalt eat the herb of the field; In the sweat
of thy face shalt thou eat bread, till thou return unto the
ground; for out of it wast thou taken: for dust thou *art,* and
unto dust shalt thou return.'."

"So, there were no thorns before Adam and Eve sinned?"
Scoefield questioned.

"There weren't." I nodded. "And Adam was a farmer. I
suppose that before he sinned, work was easy. Never again
would it be."

"You're tellin' me." Scoefield agreed.

"What about Eve and Satan?" Sarah asked.

"Eve was punished with childbirth pains. God says, in
Genesis: 'I will greatly multiply thy sorrow and thy
conception; in sorrow thou shalt bring forth children; and
thy desire *shall be* to thy husband, and he shall rule over
thee'."

"What does it mean 'thy desire *shall be* to thy husband'?"
Scoefield asked.

"I am not completely sure, actually." I answered. "We'll
have to ask Pastor Benson. That is, if you want to come to
church with me."

"Isn't that what we're havin' right now?" Scoefield asked
me. "We don't need any church. We got you, churchy-boy."

I didn't know what to say to that, so I continued with
the story. "Finally, Satan was punished. This is what the
Bible says: 'And the LORD God said unto the serpent,
Because thou hast done this, thou *art* cursed above all
cattle, and above every beast of the field; upon thy belly
shalt thou go, and dust shalt thou eat all the days of thy life:
And I will put enmity between thee and the woman, and

81

between thy seed and her seed; it shall bruise thy head, and thou shalt bruise His heel'."

"Now what in blazes does that mean?" Scoefield seemed lost.

"Well, the important part is the latter part of the verse." I said. "God was making Satan a promise. One day, a man would be born that would defeat Satan. This man would not be born of an earthly father. He would be born of a virgin woman. And His name is Jesus Christ."

That's where I stopped. Sarah and even Scoefield seemed ready for more, but it was getting late and it was a good stopping point.

"Go on, Henry." Sarah urged. "Tell us the rest."

I smiled. "I won't be able to go through the entire Bible with you in one night. We just got through the first three chapters of Genesis. There are sixty five other books to go through."

"The man has a point." Scoefield yawned. "We better get some shut-eye."

"But when will you tell us more?" Sarah pressed.

I smiled brighter, loving her desire to hear. "Tomorrow night. Promise."

"Good." She beamed. "I can't wait."

Sarah's enthusiasm did not waver at all the next day. I hated not continuing any more through the Bible with her. She was so excited to hear more and so antsy. However, I knew I had to wait for Scoefield. I wanted him to hear it just as much as Sarah. Both needed God, so I didn't dare on only telling more to Sarah. But it made me feel like a troll because she was constantly asking questions, to which I had to respond: "You'll have to wait until tonight when Scoefield gets home."

To that, she would slump, frown, groan, even glare sometimes. I felt so bad.

"Can you give me a hint?" She asked delicately as we were walking to a nearby water pump to fill the buckets.

I paused, thinking of what hint I could give. "I'm not sure how I could give you a hint without giving stuff away."

"There has to be something you can tell me!" Sarah pleaded.

"Where are we going again?" I asked her, deliberately changing the subject. I knew the answer. I just needed something else to talk about.

Sarah saw right through me. "Henry Arvin, you know full well where we're going."

"Do I?" I smiled at her. "Tell me again."

"You're changing the subject." Sarah accused, her eyes glaring.

"What makes you think that?"

"Don't you mess with me, boy." Sarah sassed. "I may be small, but I'm a Scoefield, by golly."

"Oh, and what would you do to me, big bad Scoefield?" I jested.

Sarah gazed at me with a dangerous smile. She bent low to a muddy area and grabbed a handful of mud.

I put my hands up in surrender. "Oh, no no no. Okay, you got me. I give up."

"That's what I thought." Sarah dropped the mud.

I returned to simply walking as something came to mind. "Sarah? I do have a legitimate question for you."

Sarah blinked. "What's a legita-mutt?"

I couldn't help but laugh. "It means 'real'. As in, I have a real question for you."

"Oh." Sarah replied. "Shoot."

I kept grinning, feeling clever that I had successfully changed the subject. "What do you and Scoefield do to get water in the winter?"

"We gather snow in the buckets to melt in the house." Sarah explained. "You nearly freeze your fingers off, but it's not too hard."

"Why not the water pump in the winter?" I asked. "Is it frozen?"

"No." Sarah replied. "But Scoefield doesn't like me going by myself."

"He's scared for your safety." I acknowledged.

"I know." Sarah nodded. "He loves me. But it would be a lot easier to just get water from there. Well, maybe."

"Maybe?" I asked.

Sarah shrugged. "Sometimes, the water can freeze if it gets too cold. Also, it's a long walk and the buckets hurt my hands after a while. From cold or carrying them, or both."

I chuckled a bit. "When you put it that way, gathering snow doesn't sound so bad."

Sarah giggled to herself. "I guess so."

We were nearly to the water pump, but I spotted something in the dirt.

"How about that." I said quietly to myself as I picked up the shiny items.

Fifteen pennies, and three nickels.

Thirty cents.

Sarah noticed as well. "Wow. How much did you find?"

I gave her a smile. "Thirty cents."

She raised her eyebrows. "Again?"

"It would seem so." I replied. Right or wrong, I took it as a sign from God.

I hesitated before asking Sarah what I was thinking. "What soda pop would you like tonight?"

CHAPTER SEVEN

"You should be savin' it!" Scoefield scolded me.
"Yeesh, Henry! You're a crazy spender, ya' know that?"
We were back at the malt shop. Sarah and I had gone to
Scoefield after he was done with work. We had walked
home, talking about getting soda pops again. Sarah and
Scoefield told me that I needed to save it. Eventually, I
simply stopped talking to them and purposed to get soda
pops anyway. I had asked Scoefield if just he and I could
go to the malt shop again. He came, but he was arguing
with me the whole way about how foolish I was being.
"Ya' would've had sixty cents today, Henry." He shook his
head as I ordered a lemon lime, root beer, and a cola.

"Scoefield, I want to make a deal with you." I said
suddenly.
Scoefield paused, startled by my unexpected question.
"What kind of deal?" Scoefield narrowed his eyes.
"If I can find thirty cents every week, I want you to come
to this malt shop with me every week."
Scoefield seemed surprised by this deal. "Why?"
"I enjoy our talks."
"Phht!" Scoefield scoffed. "You're a strange one, boyo.
Because my talk is oh-so educatin'."
"I'm being serious." I said sincerely. "I like our times
together. Man to man."
Scoefield stared blankly at me as our drinks were set before
us.
"Okay, so, you want gent-only-time, is that right?"
I nodded.
"With me?"

Another nod.

"You gotta' have a reason." Scoefield folded his arms.

"I want to get to know you better as a friend." I picked up our soda pops. I held out his root beer to him. "You and your sister are a few of the first friends I've ever had here. I spend a lot of time with Sarah. I want to spend time with you."

Scoefield seemed, at least a little bit, touched.

"Okay, bud."

We started heading home to Sarah. We got on the topic of hard work and all. Scoefield was talking about his diligence at work.

"That's very true." I replied to him. "You know, the Bible talks about a good work ethic."

Scoefield sighed. "Henry. I know ya' love the Bible. You talk about it all the time. But, you're about to talk more about it once we get home. Can we just...talk about somethin' else for once?"

"Sure." I told him. "Like what?"

Scoefield shrugged. "Ya' said you wanted to get to know me. How 'bout I get to know you. I mean, I feel like I barely know ya' apart from you lovin' the Bible and God and all."

"You feel you barely know me?" I was rather surprised.

"Yeah. I mean, I know your parents died and you use to be from Germany, but what else is there about you? Who is Henry Engel?"

I thought on that. *Besides the Bible, who am I?*"

"Well..." I started. "I've always wanted to be a knight."

"Ooo, there's something!" Scoefield nudged me approvingly. "Manly!"

87

I chuckled, happy that he approved of at least one of my dreams. "Well, yeah. I've always heard stories of boys who were sons of nobles and how they trained to become great men of courage, loyalty, and honor."

"Not to mention, they get all the dames." Scoefield whistled. "Slayin' them dragons and all."

I shook my head. "Those are fairy-tales. Real knights fought wars and criminals and such."

Scoefield cocked an eyebrow at me, but said nothing.

I continued. "And I love their sense of chivalry! They were taught to pledge love to only one woman, doing their best to win her and her alone. By poetry or great deeds or whatever."

Scoefield stuck his tongue out, making a 'bleah' noise. "Poetry? Get her a flower and be done with it."

"It was a more romantic time." I excused. "That's another thing about me, I suppose. I love to write things."

"Write?"

"Yes." I said. "I mean, I know you don't think writing is a manly thing to do, but I like to do it. Poetry, songs. Stuff like that."

"All-right." Scoefield laughed. "Well, we all got some girly habits, eh?"

I nudged him in the arm. "What about you, Scoefield?"

"What about me?"

"Tell me stuff about you." I answered. "I've already told you two things about me. You tell me something about you."

"What's to know?" Scoefield asked. "I work so I can live."

"That can't be all."

Scoefield pondered as we walked. "I love Sarah. She's my everythin'."

"Your everything?"

"Yeah." Scoefield nodded. "Out of all the things in this world, Sarah is the most important thing to me. I've been doin' my best to take care of her since she was a baby. Since Mama and Pop died, I've had to do a lot just to take care of her. I've had to give her 110%. I will do anythin' to protect my baby sister."

I felt something grip me in my chest at that moment. I could see that Scoefield cared for his sister more than anyone one the planet. If anything were to happen to her… or if any*one* wished to get closer to her…

"Scoefield?" I squeaked quietly.

"Hm?"

"I…like Sarah." I told him.

He glanced down at me. I glanced up at him.

Scoefield could pummel me. At any moment, if he desired, he could absolutely whup my sorry rear.

But instead…

"I know." He said.

"You do?"

"You're not exactly the best actor, Henry." Scoefield chuckled. "I knew a long time ago. I see the way you look at her. I saw how you tried to be strong for her when the Tanner boys were messin' with you two. I know ya' carry a torch for her."

So, I knew that he knew. But that was about it. I gently pressed for more information.

"So…what do you think of that?"

Scoefield scratched his chin, tossing his head side to side.

"To be honest, Henry, I wanted you as far away from her as possible. That was at the beginnin', though. I just couldn't think that my sister would get with some scrawny scamp that was more homeless than I was. And I was annoyed by ya'. What kind of guy doesn't go to get a cheap meal at a bar? And you constantly talkin' about the Bible? I thought that ya' felt you were better than me. But now? After I've seen you for who ya' are. After I've seen what a gentleman you are. After I've seen that your churchy-ness is real. I'm okay with it."

Suddenly, Scoefield grabbed my coat and pulled me close to his face. "Now, don't you get me wrong. This is *not* me givin' you permission to woo my sister. You keep your distance, boyo. She's just a friend to ya' until I give ya' the word. Ya' got me?"

"Yes." I squeaked. "Yes. I got you. I got you."

"Good." He let go of my coat.

After we walked a bit, took sips from our soda pops a bit, I piped up again. "I mean, I was going to ask. I just don't really know how to do any of that sort of thing. My father never taught me this."

"Well, I don't know either." Scoefield replied. "So, we could just figure it out together, eh? Let's just go really slow, okay? For my sake."

"You make it sound like it's a done deal." I laughed. "I mean, we don't even know if she likes me back."

"Correction." Scoefield commented. "*You* don't even know she likes you back."

I stopped walking for a moment. "What are you saying?"

Scoefield turned around with a grin on his face. "Churchy-boy, not only do *I* know that she likes you, but so does *everyone* else."

My heart started beating extremely fast. At the same time, I felt like my feet were lifting off the ground.

Apparently, Scoefield could see it too. "Calm down, Henry. Remember, ***nothin'*** is happenin' between you two yet."
"She likes me?" I ran up to him, talking a mile a minute. "Did she tell you or did you just find out? How long have you known? What do you mean everyone else knows?"
Scoefield put his hand over his eyes as he shook his head. "You really are a girl."

Scoefield turned to me and placed his hands on my shoulders.
"Henry, listen to me." He said in a serious tone. "Sarah is a beautiful, wonderful girl. She reminds me a lot of my mama. But my mama made a really lousy decision: she married my pop. Now, people tell me that my pop seemed like a real charmer. A real nice guy. But he wasn't. He was angry and he was cruel and he was a drunk. And my mama died because of that. She lived a horrible life after she married my pop. I don't want that for Sarah. I want Sarah to have the best life she can. I want her happy and taken care of. If that is with you, I'll let it happen. But remember what I said earlier? I feel like I barely know ya'. I want to make sure you are the guy for her. Until then, you will not touch her, you will not tell her lovey-dovey stuff, you will not do anythin' of that sort without my permission. You understand? I like ya', Henry. I think you're a nice guy. But I want the best man marryin' my sister. I want an honorable man, a good man to marry her. You gotta' prove that you're worthy of her. And don't tell her any of this. This is between you and me. If you show me that you are the man I hope you are, I'll let you court her. Until then, stay where you are. Can ya' do that for me?"
I nodded. "Absolutely."

91

"You're back!" Sarah exclaimed. "Henry, what happened next! What happened after God made his threat to Satan?"

I smiled. I was so happy to see Sarah eager to hear the story of the Bible. But after the talk I had with Scoefield, I was really just happy to see Sarah.

"Hi, Sarah." I said with a very happy, gentle smile. Scoefield noticed it and punched me in the arm.

"Right." I winced. "Yes, the story. Let me get my Bible. Sarah looked rather concerned at Scoefield. Scoefield sat down with an unapologetic smile on as he tossed Sarah her cola.

"You shouldn't punch him." Sarah growled quietly as she caught her drink.

"He needs to toughen up." Scoefield retorted. "You should be thankin' me. I'm just helpin' him along."

"So." I interrupted, looking in my Bible. "We left off around Genesis 3:20."

"Yes." Sarah responded. "God has just told Satan, Adam, and Eve their punishments for their sins."

"Right." I smiled at her. "So, because Adam and Eve sinned, the had to be driven out of the Garden of Eden."

"The snake too, right?" Scoefield asked.

I was about to say "yes", when I looked back at my Bible. "Actually." I blinked. "It just says that Adam and Eve were driven out of the Garden."

Scoefield raised an eyebrow. "The snake gets off easy?"

"No. I just don't know." I replied. "The Bible doesn't say that Satan was driven out of the Garden. I'll have to ask my Pastor."

I continued with the story. "Anyway, Adam and Eve had to live their days out of God's presence. Now they had

92

to work harder than they ever had before and they were now imperfect beings. Sinners. Just like us today. But Adam and Eve had two sons. Cain and Abel. Cain was the firstborn, Abel was the second. Cain became a tiller of the ground, a farmer. Just like his father. Abel became a shepherd. And in those days, people gave sacrifices, offerings, to God."

Scoefield and Sarah both gave me bizarre looks.

"I know. I know. It sounds…barbaric. But, it was what they did."

"And God was okay with that?" Sarah asked. "You mean that they killed animals and God wanted that?"

"It was a symbol of what was to come, Sarah." I explained. "'Without shedding of blood is no remission'. Jesus would later sacrifice Himself as a lamb. The sacrifices beforehand were to symbolize that. Be a picture of it."

They both stared at me blankly.

"You'll understand it later." I told them. "Anyway, Cain and Abel. They both brought offerings to God. Cain from the fruit of the ground. Abel from his flock of sheep. It says here that 'And the LORD had respect unto Abel and to his offering: But unto Cain and to his offering he had not respect'."

"What?" Scoefield interjected. "God doesn't like fruit?"

"Maybe He doesn't." Sarah answered Scoefield. "The sin dealt with fruit, too."

"There are different views on why God didn't have respect towards Cain's offering." I replied. "The Bible doesn't give us the definite reason, but some assume that it was because Cain wasn't living a righteous life, that he didn't have a heart that was devoted to God."

93

Then I stopped for a moment and gave a small chuckle.
"Others say that it was Cain brought fruit as an offering."
"Called it." Scoefield smirked. "God doesn't like fruit."
"It's not that." I told him. "People believe that because God desires blood sacrifices."
"Hey, it's fine, boyo." Scoefield grinned. "I won't hold it against God that He don't like fruit. He's wants meat. I'm all for that. I don't like fruit either. Bring on the steak."
I laughed at that. "I see. So, back to the story. Cain was upset by this. Very upset. He became angry. And God noticed this. God said to Cain 'Why art thou wroth? and why is thy countenance fallen?'. That basically means 'Why are you so angry?'. God was trying to show Cain that he had no real reason to be so angry. Then God says 'If thou doest well, shalt thou not be accepted? And if thou doest not well, sin lieth at the door. And unto thee *shall be* his desire, and thou shalt rule over him'."
"Now what does that mean?" Sarah asked.
"God is laying out the consequences of what Cain will do next." I explained. "God is saying if he does well, he will be accepted. But if he doesn't, sin is waiting for him. Then, God switches over to the heart of Cain's anger: Abel."
"Cain was angry at Abel?" Sarah asked.
"Yes." I said. "Cain brought his sacrifice, but it wasn't accepted for whatever reason. Abel's was. How humiliating for the older brother to be rejected but the little brother to be accepted. Cain was angry at his brother. So, God talks to Cain about it. 'And unto thee *shall be* his desire, and thou shalt rule over him'. God was saying that Abel still respected Cain as his older brother. He had not lost any respect from Abel. And God was saying that Cain would rule over him, as to say 'You are the firstborn. You have authority over your younger brother'."

"Preach that." Scoefield said as he nudged Sarah. Sarah, in return, hit him in the arm.

I continued. "But Cain would not listen to reason. He kept his anger. He held on to it. And he went to his brother, out in a field, to talk to him."

I sighed. "Abel never left that field."

A solemn silence suddenly broke out in our small shack.

"Whoa." Scoefield said, eyes wide.

Sarah simply placed her hand to her mouth. "Cain…he…?"

"Cain slew his brother." I breathed out. "The first murderer."

"That's so awful." Sarah shook her head. "What did Adam and Eve do?"

"Hold on, hold on." I told her. "First, God was the one who went to Cain. It says here 'And the LORD said unto Cain, Where *is* Abel thy brother? And he said, I know not: *Am* I my brother's keeper? And he said, What hast thou done? the voice of thy brother's blood crieth unto me from the ground. And now *art* thou cursed from the earth, which hath opened her mouth to receive thy brother's blood from thy hand; When thou tillest the ground, it shall not henceforth yield unto thee her strength; a fugitive and a vagabond shalt thou be in the earth. And Cain said unto the LORD, My punishment *is* greater than I can bear. Behold, thou hast driven me out this day from the face of the earth; and from thy face shall I be hid; and I shall be a fugitive and a vagabond in the earth; and it shall come to pass, *that* every one that findeth me shall slay me. And the LORD said unto him, Therefore whosoever slayeth Cain, vengeance shall be taken on him sevenfold. And the LORD set a mark upon Cain, lest any finding him should kill him.

And Cain went out from the presence of the LORD, and dwelt in the land of Nod, on the east of Eden'."

I stopped reading to see if Scoefield or Sarah needed any explanation. Both of them were simply waiting.

"To kill someone in your own family." Sarah whispered. "How could someone do that?"

"Okay, that's enough for tonight." Scoefield suddenly said. "Put the book away. Let's be done with it for tonight."

I was rather startled by his reaction. "But Scoefield, we're about to get to the good news."

"I don't care." Scoefield seemed almost angry. "We've read enough."

"But Bradley." Sarah turned to him. "I want to hear more. I want to hear the good news. Don't you?"

"You know what?" Scoefield gritted his teeth. "Fine. You two read. I'm goin' out for some air."

Scoefield quickly stood up and moved for the door.

"But Scoefield-" I tried to say.

He slammed the door behind him.

I glanced over at Sarah. I simply gave a look of confusion.

She shrugged. "Don't look at me. I have no idea what that was."

"Did I say something I shouldn't have?" I asked her.

"I don't think so." Sarah glanced at the door. "Maybe it was what I said."

"What do you mean?" I asked.

"I was talking about how Cain killed Abel. He's probably thinking about how Pop…"

She didn't have to finish. "Oh."

Sarah nodded. "Scoefield was there when they crashed. It must still be very traumatic for him."

"What about you, Sarah?"

She gazed right into my eyes. "It's hard. Very hard. I'm growing up in a shack with my older brother. I don't have a father that will love me and protect me. I don't have a mother that will teach me how to be a lady and help me find my place in this world. Our parents…they surely weren't perfect. Our father was a very wicked man. But I still want him back. I'd give almost anything to have them back."

"I understand." I said. "I never thought I would be without my parents this early in life. I thought that my parents would die in a good, old age. It was so sudden. All I have are the memories of them. How they lived."

Then I took a deep breath. "But we're not hopeless, Sarah."

Sarah raised her eyebrows slightly.

"God." I pointed to my Bible. "He's not just a story. He is real. He loves all of us. I'm in His sovereign hands. And you can be too."

Sarah looked confused. "What do you mean?"

I opened the Bible again to where I stopped. "Cain. He was wicked, right?"

"Yes."

"Well, so are you." I said gingerly. "So am I. As I said before, we are all sinners. All of us are wicked. And God is holy, remember?"

"I remember." She nodded.

"And holiness and wickedness cannot be together. It is like putting darkness with light. It can't be done. Light consumes darkness and darkness flees from light. There is no mixture. So, God has to place sinners somewhere out of His presence. In a place that will give us what we truly deserve. Sin needs to be punished, remember? Like a murderer needs to be punished for what he's done."

I began flipping through the Bible.

"Romans 6:23 – 'For the wages of sin *is* death'. Sarah, you and I and everybody on earth have judgment on our heads. Because of our sin, we are supposed to die."

I could see conviction, fear, and anxiety on Sarah's face. The Holy Spirit was working.

"*Please, God.*" I prayed silently. "*Let her be saved tonight.*"

"What do you mean 'die'?" Sarah whispered.

"Hell." I told her.

Sarah swallowed nervously.

"God created hell for Satan and his demons." I explained. "It is a place of torture and nightmares. All who go there burn in a fire that cannot be put out. They are eaten by worms that cannot be squished. They-"

"Stop, Henry." Sarah exclaimed, shaking with fear. "Don't tell me this. Please don't tell me this. I don't want to know what this place is."

"Okay." I nodded. "The point is, all of mankind is headed there too."

"Everyone?" Sarah gasped.

"Yes. It's what sin has done to us."

"How do I get rid of it?" Sarah asked, panic in her voice. "There has to be a way to get rid of sin or to do something to be good or anything!"

"There is nothing *we* can do." I told her. Then I smiled. "But God did something."

I read Romans 6:23 again. "'For the wages of sin is death *but* the gift of God *is* eternal life through Jesus Christ our Lord.'"

Sarah blinked, not entirely understanding. "What is the gift? How do I get the gift?"

I was so ready to just tell her. But I stayed patient. "Let me read you another passage."

I flipped to Isaiah 53:2 – 8. "'For He shall grow up before Him as a tender plant, and as a root out of a dry ground: He hath no form nor comeliness; and when we shall see Him, *there is* no beauty that we should desire Him. He is despised and rejected of men; a man of sorrows, and acquainted with grief: and we hid as it were *our* faces from Him; He was despised, and we esteemed Him not. Surely He hath borne our griefs, and carried our sorrows: yet we did esteem Him stricken, smitten of God, and afflicted. But He *was* wounded for our transgressions, *He was* bruised for our iniquities: the chastisement of our peace *was* upon Him; and with His stripes we are healed. All we like sheep have gone astray; we have turned every one to his own way; and the LORD hath laid on Him the iniquity of us all. He was oppressed, and He was afflicted, yet He opened not his mouth: He is brought as a lamb to the slaughter, and as a sheep before her shearers is dumb, so He openeth not His mouth. He was taken from prison and from judgment: and who shall declare His generation? for He was cut off out of the land of the living: for the transgression of my people was He stricken'."
Sarah shook her head slightly. "What does that mean?"
I moved closer to her and sat down beside her. "Sarah. God knows we are sinners and that we are destined for hell. So, God sent His Son, Jesus Christ, to earth as a man. Jesus was born of a virgin and, being God, never sinned once. He lived a sinless life and yet was killed for crimes that He had never committed."
"Why?"

"Because He was being a sacrifice for us." I smiled "Remember how I told you that the sacrifices were a picture? They were a picture of what was going to happen with Jesus. He, being perfect and innocent, died for those who were corrupt and wicked. Jesus paid the penalty of death for us so we would never have to pay it. He then rose up from the dead as our risen Saviour and sits on the right hand of God in heaven to this very day."

"So we don't have to go to hell?" Sarah took a sigh of relief.

"We don't." I acknowledged. "But God never forces anything on anyone. He has the gift of life. The way to escape hell is offered freely to us."

I picked up my Bible and held it out to her. Sarah gave me a questioning look.

"It's like this. I am holding out my Bible to you. But it is not yours until you take it, right?"

She nodded in comprehension.

"That's exactly what it is with Jesus and the gift of salvation. The price is paid. The gift is yours. Just take it, Sarah."

She placed her hands on the Bible. "But Henry…how do I take the gift?"

"Prayer." I told her. "You ask God for it. You ask Jesus to forgive you of your sins and acknowledge that He is God. It says in Romans 10:9 – 10 'That if thou shalt confess with thy mouth the Lord Jesus, and shalt believe in thine heart that God hath raised him from the dead, thou shalt be saved. For with the heart man believeth unto righteousness; and with the mouth confession is made unto salvation'."

"I want to do it." Sarah said immediately. "I want to be saved. Please help me, Henry."

"*Thank you, God.*" I prayed. "*Now help me lead this girl to You.*"

"Bow your head. Close your eyes." I told Sarah.

She did so. I did as well.

"Now, I'm not going to pray for you." I told her. "I want you to talk to God. Tell Him your heart. Ask Him to forgive you and save you, Sarah."

Several moments passed of silence. Then I heard her speak.

"Hello, God. My name is Sarah Scoefield. I'm…not too familiar with any of this. I never learned much about You until Henry came along. But I know that I'm a wicked sinner. Something in my heart is telling me that. I know that what Henry has said is absolutely true. I don't know how I know that, but I do. I also know that it's true what Henry said about Jesus Christ. Again, I don't know how I know it, but something inside me is telling me that Jesus Christ did come to earth and He did die and He did rise again. I believe that. God, I want You to forgive me of all the bad things I have done. I know that I don't see them as very bad, but I know that You are holy and You can't tolerate them. Even if it was something like eating fruit that should not have been eaten. God, I don't want to go to hell. I want to live in heaven after I die. Please, God. Don't let me go to hell. I want to be saved."

Suddenly I felt a nudge. I opened my left eye to see Sarah peeking at me with her right eye.

"What do I do now?" She whispered, as if she didn't want God to hear it. "Did I do it right?"

I chuckled. "Amen. Yes, Sarah."

I turned to her, smiling brightly. "You have been saved by the blood of Jesus Christ."

I can't explain the kind of joy and relief I found in that girl's eyes at that moment. She was so overwhelmed with the fact that she was saved that she began crying, throwing her arms around me and embracing me tightly.

I had a massive mix of emotions as well. I had just led someone to the Lord for the first time. Because of God working through me, Sarah Scoefield would never see the flames of hell. I was overjoyed simply at that fact. Not to mention how happy I was after seeing how joyous she was to get the weight of eternity off of her shoulders. But I also really liked this girl. And she was hugging me very tightly. I knew I was red in the face and butterflies were swarming in my chest. At the same time, I could hear Scoefield's words to me earlier that night:

"I want to make sure you are the guy for her. Until then, ***you will not touch her***"

I gulped. I was terrified to think what Scoefield would do if he walked in at that moment.

"It's okay." I thought to myself. *"She hugged you. You didn't touch her, she touched you."*

Regardless, I made sure the hug was over quickly.

CHAPTER EIGHT

When Scoefield did return, Sarah refused to stop talking about how she had been saved. She was telling Scoefield everything and how wonderful it all was. The whole time, Scoefield was looking at her like she was crazy. Then he would look at me with a questioning glare, as if to say "What did you do?"

Then he would look back at her. He repeated this until Sarah changed subjects.

"Bradley!" She suddenly exclaimed. "*You* need to get saved!"

"Eh, no." Scoefield immediately shot her down.

"Yes!" Sarah pleaded. "Jesus is holding out the gift of salvation to you! You need to take it! Henry, tell him!"

"Actually." Scoefield eyed me. "I would like to have a little chat with Henry. Come with me, pally."

Scoefield grabbed me by my collar and drug me outside.

"Sarah, stay here." He told his sister before closing the door. Then he gave me the same questioning glare he had been giving me.

"Yes?" I asked, rather afraid.

"What did ya' do?" He glared. "What did ya' tell her?"

"Exactly what she said." I answered.

"Henry, are ya' for real?"

"Pardon?"

"Are ya' for real?" Scoefield asked again. "Or are ya' just tryin' to get closer to my sister?"

"What? Not at all." I told him.

Scoefield shook his head. "Henry, I've seen churchy people. Some of em' are good people. They believe all that fairy-tale junk. But some of em'…"

103

He eyed me again. "Are just after somethin'."

"I *do* believe in everything I told her." I assured Scoefield. "I believe in everything I've told you."

"How do I know that?" Scoefield questioned me. "It seems mighty iffy of you to suddenly get her all excited on the night that I told ya' she liked you."

"It is coincidence only, Scoefield." I told him.

"So what happens now?" Scoefield continued with the questions. "She's 'saved'. Does she start goin' to church with you?"

In truth, Sarah had already gone to church with me most Sundays. She would fall asleep every church service, but she did go. I thought on that and decided it best not to inform Scoefield of that at that particular time.

"Yes, I suppose so." I said.

"Oh really?" Scoefield glared. "You tryin' to get her alone, are ya'?"

"No." I shook my head frantically. "We wouldn't be alone. My church has a lot of people in it. You know, if you were really concerned about her, you could come with-"

"I aint goin' to church, Henry." Scoefield stomped his foot. "I went a couple of times. It's a bore. The churchy people look at ya' like you're a monster. There's hardly any real compassion there."

"I'm sorry." I said genuinely. "My church isn't like that. Well, I mean, you may find it boring but I really enjoy-"

"Henry, I want this to stop." Scoefield interrupted again. "I can handle a nice bedtime story every night. What I don't want is you throwin' up God everywhere, ya' hear me?"

"Okay, okay." I told him.

"Good." Scoefield finished. He then opened up the door and went inside.

I stayed outside for a minute. I gazed up at the stars. "You're really starting to get to him." I prayed in German. "But he's rejecting You. Please break through to him, Lord. Like you did with Sarah."

I decided to give Scoefield a break. We continued our malt shops visits, but I put the Bible down for a while. I felt it was best at the time. It may not have been, but that's what I did. Sarah was upset at it, but she respected my decision. It wasn't until one winter morning when I began planning on bringing back the Bible devotions. I woke up early, as was usual. Before sun up and before Scoefield was awake. I took that time to pray and read my Bible. By the time I was done, Scoefield was up and getting ready for work.

"Take care of her." He told me before leaving. "But don't ya' dare do anythin' that your God wouldn't want you to." As he left, I pondered on where this new adversity had come from. Over the months, even without me "throwing up God everywhere", Scoefield seemed to see me as untrustworthy, especially with his sister. Of course, we both knew that I did have affections for Sarah and that I was indeed a man with sinful passions, like every other man. But I had not given him any reason to believe I was going to be anything but a gentleman towards Sarah. However, Scoefield had anger towards church-goers. Claiming them all to be hypocritical. Perhaps he thought I was.

"Good morning." Sarah broke me from my thoughts as she sat up on the mattress.

I smiled. "*Guten morgen*, Sarah."

She gave a questioning smile. "Is that German?"

"You would be correct." I answered.

"It sounds rather bland." Sarah laughed.

"Maybe it is, but many Germans feel that the American language is sloppy."

"Sloppy, huh?" Sarah chuckled. "Well, we are not the cleanest right now. Speaking of which…um, Henry? Could you go outside? I need to do some girl things."

Without any question, I went outside. I had no idea what 'girl things' were but I had no intention to find out. I waited outside for about forty minutes, pacing back and forth to keep myself warm. I gazed around at the other shacks that were in our little Hooverville. Many women and children were out, gathering snow into buckets and pans. No doubt, it was for water. That's what we did too. It was easier than walking all the way to the water pump in the cold. It was rather important to get clean snow instead of the smudgy, dirt-filled kind. We had three buckets, which was nice. They were decent sized. About big enough to hold a small dog. We would fill one, let it sit for a couple days in the shack so the snow would melt. As we used that water, we would fill the other buckets with snow and wait for them to melt. It wasn't ideal, but it worked for us. Sarah finally opened the door.

"You can come in now." She informed me, quickly pulling herself back inside.

As I came in, I noticed that she had a different change of clothes on and her skin and hair were somewhat wet.

"Could you dump that bucket of water out?" She pointed as she brushed her hair.

I did so. "Did you just wash yourself?"

"Mm-hmm." She answered. "I don't usually wash in the mornings. At least, not in winter. It's dangerous."

"Dangerous?"

"Yes, because of the cold." She explained. "This shack is warmer than outside, but not that much warmer. If you're wet, you could really get sick. That's why Scoefield and I usually wash ourselves when the other is here. By the way, I'll need you to do something for me."

"What would that be?" I asked.

I then noticed that Sarah was getting back under the blankets on the bed.

"I need you to…" She was blushing. "Hug me underneath the blankets."

Now I was blushing. "What?"

"This is why someone needs to be around when we wash." Sarah was avoiding eye-contact. "I need to get dry so I don't get sick. Until then, I need you to keep me warm."

Very logical. It was frigid out, she was wet from washing, she needed extra body heat.

I completely understood. But in my heart, something felt wrong. And Scoefield's words echoed in my head:

"Don't ya' dare do anythin' that your God wouldn't want you to."

I couldn't help but think that it wasn't coincidence. The very day I was thinking of bringing back our Bible reading, something…questionable came up.

"Is that okay?" Sarah interrupted my thoughts. "I know it's rather awkward."

I took a deep breath. This was out of need, not pleasure. "Yes, it is. But, I'll do it."

I slipped under the blankets with her and hugged her close. She was warm, but I could feel her shaking.

"Oh brrrr!" She shivered when I hugged her. "You're freezing!"

"Sorry." I muttered. "I was just outside."

107

"Should have thought that one through, huh?" She laughed.

"I suppose so."

We didn't have much genuine conversation. Every time we tried to start some, it would die quickly. We continually ran out of things to say.

So, we eventually stopped trying. We lied there, holding one another. My head was thinking a million different thoughts. Some were about how…in all honesty…how pleasant it was. I was holding the girl I fancied in my arms. She was leaning her head against me. It was truly very nice. On the other hand, I was conflicted within. Was this the sort of conduct that I, as a Christian, should have been partaking in? Truth, it wasn't a flippant decision. She did need to be kept warm. Sickness was real. And yes, it wasn't my fault that she suddenly threw this on me. She should have asked beforehand.

But still…what we were doing…was affecting us emotionally. Passions were being lit. Fires were starting. We were beginning something that was very dangerous.

"I'm think I'm dry enough now." Sarah finally spoke.

"Okay." Was all I said in response. We awkwardly broke away from each other and slipped off the bed. For several minutes, neither of us knew what to say and we didn't try to bring up conversation.

"Well, then what would you like to do today?" Sarah finally broke the silence.

I was without any ideas. "I'm not sure. What do you think?"

Sarah shrugged her shoulders. "We could just try and clean up around here."

I glanced around at the small shack we sat it. "How long does that usually take."

"I can clean everything before the fastest horse could run a lap at the races." Sarah laughed.

"I bet." I smiled. "Well, then, I don't suppose we'll stick around doing that. Why don't we go find something to do."

"Find something to do?" Sarah gave a skeptical look. "In the middle of *this* weather? What's your plan? Catch colds?"

"I'm German." I grinned. "I lived much further north than here. German winters are far worse than these measly American ones."

"Okay then, Big Shot." Sarah smirked. "You can just go enjoy this 'measly' winter weather by yourself then because I don't think I want to go outside."

"Oh, come on." I threw out my hands. "What are we supposed to do in here. Sleep?"

Sarah shrugged. "What's wrong with sleeping?"

"It's boring." I told her. "And we would be wasting a wonderful day."

Sarah groaned. "Well, what would we do out there?"

"If we don't find anything, we can sing on the street corner." I told her. "That way, at the very least, we're making money."

Sarah looked at me for a moment.

Then she groaned again.

"Where is everyone?" I asked as we aimlessly walked down the streets. Hardly anyone was around.

"Hmm, let's see." Sarah began sarcastically. "It's only 9:00 A.M., it's *freezing* out – gee, I *wonder* where everyone is. Probably inside, like we should be."

"No need to have such a dismal attitude, Sarah." I told her. "God can do something amazing out today. If we were inside, we would miss it."

"I'm pretty sure that if God wanted something to happen with us, He could very easily do it while we are in a warm place."

Suddenly, Sarah grabbed my hand and started pulling me towards a hotel.

"That being said." She muttered. "We are going inside before I die of frostbite."

I should have been more surprised at how strong she was in proportion to her size. I mean, she was nearly dragging me towards the hotel.

But all I could think about was that she was holding my hand.

We entered a very nice hotel. We were instantly buffeted by a wave of warmth. Both Sarah and I gave a breath of relief.

I began looking around. For some reason, even in the nation's current state of poverty, this hotel was thriving. People in very fancy and expensive apparel moved here and there. Past the hotel desk was an open area with couches and chairs that looked soft, comfortable, and very inviting. There was a massive fireplace with a large but gentle fire burning inside it. Next to the fireplace was a Christmas tree.

"Wow." I whispered. I began to walk towards the fireplace to get a bit warmer.

"What're you doing?" Sarah whispered at me.

"What?" I turned around to her. "I'm just getting closer to the fire."

"They won't let us." Sarah frowned. "They're probably about to-"

"Excuse me." A tall man in a suit approached us. "Children, where are your parents?"

I hated that question.

The man looked very proper. He had perfect standing posture, which made him look all the taller. He had an oval face with a very pointed nose. His eyes seemed accusational as they glowered at us from down his nose. As he came close to us, he put a handkerchief to his nose, indirectly telling us that we looked and smelled revolting to him.

Sarah walked up behind me and took my hand. I could tell by the way she hid behind me that she was scared.

"We're orphans, sir." I told him politely.

"Orphans?" He pursed his lips. "Then you have no business here. I must ask you to leave."

I was rather shocked by his sudden dismissal. "Sir, we were simply just going to get a little warm before-"

"Customers only are allowed to use this fine establishment as a place of refuge from the weather." The man interrupted. "If we were to house every street urchin that came to our doorstep, this hotel would be infested with whatever they brought along with them, the expenses would be far higher than income, and we would be shut down. Now, leave or I will have you thrown out."

That was that. Sarah and I left.

We stood right outside the doors. The cold wind seemed far more bitter now, considering we had been in the warmth.

111

"You're still new to this, aren't you?" Sarah asked me after a few moments of silence.

"I shouldn't be." I whispered. "I was homeless in Germany. But we weren't treated like we were rats. Everyone was poor."

We sat in silence for a couple minutes longer.

"Come on." I told Sarah. "You were right. Let's just go back to the house and-"

I was stopped by a sudden commotion coming from inside the hotel. Within moments, the door burst open and two hotel employees threw a man out on the sidewalk. As soon as he landed, they slammed the doors closed.

"I told you I'll pay you tomorrow!" The man slowly got to his feet. "Scumbags!"

The man was rather large. Fat, to be blunt. His voice sounded like an automobile engine with gravel in it. His clothes, however, looked very expensive. Underneath his very nice coat was a suit that wasn't unlike the man's who asked us to leave. On his balding scalp, he wore a bowler hat.

"*They throw out even rich people.*" I thought to myself.

It was at that moment that the man noticed Sarah and I.

"Can you believe them?" He growled.

We remained silent.

"Did they throw you out too?" He asked us.

"Not exactly." I replied. "But we were asked to leave."

"Just because you're dirty, right?" The man shook his head with a scowl. Then he cursed. Right in front of us.

"Sir." I said firmly.

"What?"

"There is a lady present." I gestured to Sarah.

"Oh, Henry, stop." Sarah whispered to me. "I'm hardly a-"

"I ask that you apologize." I told the man.

112

The man stared at us for a couple moments, his eyes flicking back and forth between Sarah and me. After several moments of silence, the man tipped his hat. "My apologies, ma'am." He said kindly. "You're right. I shouldn't swear like that."
"Thank you." I told him.

The man looked at me again, this time with a peculiar expression. "Have I met you two before?"
I had never seen the man before. "No."
I glanced at Sarah. She simply shook her head to me.
"I don't believe so, sir." I told him.
He tapped his foot as he looked at us. "I swear, I've seen you two before. I know it. Now where did I see you?"
"I go to the diner on 37th street." Sarah spoke up. "My brother works there."
"That's not it." He shook his head. Then, it was like a light-bulb came on for the man.
"You're the girl who sings!" He pointed at Sarah. "Every night. And then you sang that song. That really special song!"
"Never?" I realized. He was there when Sarah and I met. He heard my song.
"That was some real talent, kid." The man told Sarah. "Where did you get that song?"
"Henry wrote it for me." Sarah looked to me.
"You wrote it?" The man's face became serious. "You wrote that song?"
I simply nodded.
The man began tapping his foot again. Much more rapidly this time.
"Where are your parents?" He asked suddenly.

We didn't even have to say anything this time. The mix of sorrow and frustration on our faces told him the answer.

"I see." He said not so sympathetically. "What if I told you kids I got an opportunity for you?"

"What kind of opportunity?" I asked.

CHAPTER NINE

"A fat man in a bowler hat?" Scoefield asked us. "Named Wesley Butters?"

We had gone to Scoefield immediately after we had talked with Mr. Butters. Luckily, the diner wasn't so busy so Scoefield could take a break to talk with us.

"He said he works for a recording studio." Sarah told Scoefield. "And he wants me to sing the song Henry wrote."

"To be put on the radio?" Scoefield raised his eyebrows.

Sarah nodded. "He says he can make us a lot of money."

"What's the catch?" Scoefield squinted.

"I don't see any, Bradley."

"There's gotta' be a catch." Scoefield clicked his tongue. "I mean, the guy's name is Butters? **Butters**? Sounds sketchy to me."

"He did get thrown out of a fancy hotel." I mentioned.

"Did ya' say yes to 'im?" Scoefield asked us.

"We told him we needed to think about it." Sarah explained.

"Good." Scoefield nodded. "Bring him over around 3:00. I'll talk to him on my break."

"He's actually right outside." I commented.

"What?"

"He drove us here." Sarah said. "He's waiting for us to make a decision."

"What a creep." Scoefield wrinkled his nose. "Has he been followin' ya'?"

"He was very persistent." I told Scoefield.

Scoefield sighed. "Bring him in. But let *me* do *all* of the talkin'. You both got that?"

Sarah and I nodded.

I brought in Mr. Butters.

"This is Scoefield." I told Mr. Butters. "He's Sarah's older brother."

"Mr. Scoefield, how are you, young sir?" Mr. Butters held out his hand.

Scoefield just stared at him. "Don't call me 'Mr. Scoefield'. Just Scoefield to ya', pally."

Mr. Butters said nothing, still holding out his hand.

"I ain't gonna' shake it." Scoefield said firmly. "I need to keep my hands clean and I don't know what kind of dirt ya' been in."

Mr. Butters slowly let down his hand. "I see. No formalities, then."

"None."

"Well then, let's just get to the chase." Mr. Butters sat down. "I want your sister and her friend to write songs and sing them for me."

"Write songs?" Scoefield eyed him. "I thought they said you just wanted them to sing one."

"That was the original plan, yes." Mr. Butters nodded. "But on the way here, I discovered Mr. Engel has quite the talent with songwriting. This could be a possible career for him. I can make all of you a great deal of money."

"A great deal of money usually comes at a great deal of cost." Scoefield folded his arms. "What's the catch, *Butters*?"

Mr. Butters' foot began to tap. "No catch."

"There's always one."

"Not this time."

"What do ya' take me for?"

"Your sister and friend will get to do what they love and get paid for it at the same time."

"But you're leavin' something out."

Mr. Butters began to get irritated. "All-right, son, look. I need them."

"No, you *want* them." Scoefield corrected.

"No, I do *need* them." Mr. Butters pushed.

"Why?"

"Because I'll get fired if they don't help me." Mr. Butters sighed, his foot no longer tapping.

Scoefield softened up, but still eyed him suspiciously. "Explain yourself."

"I work for a recording studio." He began. "We were doing famously, and still are, but times are tough. I need something new, something fresh, something reviving. And, up until today, I was set with that. I had talent with both singing and writing, but they walked out on me for a better offer. So, I'm losing money fast. If I'm going to stay out of the Hoovervilles, I need someone who can sing and someone who can write songs."

Mr. Butters gestured to Sarah and I. "I saw these two sing nearly a year ago. Back then, I didn't need them. Now, I do. And they're good at what I'm asking them to do. Trust me, you will get a substantial amount of money if they come and work for me."

"And if you start cheatin' us?" Scoefield questioned.

"I wouldn't."

"How can we trust you won't?"

"You can't." Mr. Butters said bluntly. "But even if I did cheat you out some money, you would still be making much more than you are right now."

Mr. Butters leaned closer to Scoefield. "You're not homeless on the streets, but you still could use the extra money I'm offering you."

Scoefield stared coldly at him. He stood there staring at Mr. Butters for the longest time until…

"They can sing the first song." Scoefield said. "We'll see how that goes. See if we like it. Then we'll go on from there."

Mr. Butters was satisfied with that. "Thank you."

Scoefield kept his cold stare on Mr. Butters. "If you double-cross us, I know cops that will turn a blind eye to what I'll do to you." Scoefield threatened. "So watch yourself…**Butters**."

"Not the friendliest kid." Mr. Butters mentioned as we rode in his car. We were on our way to the recording studio. Apparently, we were going to sing that very day.

"He's been through much." I replied to him from the back seat. I noticed out of the corner of my eye that Sarah was scooting awfully close to me. I was pretty certain it was because she wasn't too comfortable being in Mr. Butters' car. He was a complete stranger to us.

I rested my hand on top of hers. Sarah immediately began blushing and glanced right into my eyes.

"It'll be okay." I mouthed to her.

"We have all been through much, son." Mr. Butters continued the conversation. "Hoover threw all of America in this-"

He cursed again. He used the Lord's name in vain.

"Mr. Butters." I furrowed my brow. "That is my God you just used as a curse word. I would appreciate it if you didn't do that."

Mr. Butters looked at me through the rear-view mirror. "Oh! Do forgive me. It's a nasty habit of mine. You kids church-goers or something?"

"Yes." I told him.

Mr. Butters sighed. "I should really get back in church."

"We would love to have you at Bible Baptist Church, if you want to come." I invited.

"I just might." Mr. Butters nodded. "Oh, we're here."

We pulled up to a tall building in downtown New York City. As we stepped out, Sarah and I gazed at how high the building seemed to reach up towards the gray clouds above.

"Come along now." Mr. Butters told us as he walked to the front doors.

The size of the building put us in wonderment, but it sure was stranger on the inside. As we walked through the lobby of the building, I noted how it all seemed very busy and business-like. Nothing like a hotel or a restaurant. People in suits walking here and there, paying no mind to us. All conversation seemed to be about some type of things that Sarah and I didn't understand. We passed the front desk where women sat answering phone calls. They were constantly saying "hold, please" and "I'll connect you right away". We turned to the left to find a series of elevators. As we reached the elevator, it occurred to me that I had never been in a business-building before. No wonder it seemed so foreign. Sarah and I walked to the middle of the elevator as Mr. Butters pressed the "19" button. Before we knew it, however, six other people clamored to get in the same elevator that Sarah, Mr. Butters, and I were in. Sarah and I were forced to the back of the elevator as multiple people stuffed themselves in. Mr. Butters worked the buttons for everyone.

"Which floor for you, ma'am?"

"Sixteen, please."

"I'm on twenty-four."

"And you, sir?"

"Eight."

"There you are."

"Thank you."

I had never felt so uncomfortably out of place in my life. It was even more peculiar that none of the adults even regarded us. In the hotel, we were noticed immediately, in a negative sense. Here, we might as well have been invisible. I glanced at Sarah to see that she seemed to be feeling the exact same as me.

The worst part was that no one said anything for the entire time we were on the elevator. For nineteen floors, Sarah and I just awkwardly looked at our shoes as the elevator stopped, people left, other people got on, and the elevator started moving again.

After what seemed like generations, we reached floor nineteen.

The recording studio.

We stepped off the elevator to find an immaculate hallway that led to a single desk. The desk was occupied by three women. Two were typing on typewriters and the third was answering calls. Mr. Butters hurriedly led us past the desk to the rooms behind, where music could faintly be heard.

"Good afternoon, Mr. Butters." One of the ladies on the typewriter said. She peered at Sarah and I as we were walking past her. "Who are these-?"

"Let's hope it is a good afternoon, Barbara." Mr. Butters interrupted, leading us to a door behind the ladies' desk. Behind the door was another hallway, but this one was different. On the left and on the right were rooms where musicians and singers were found performing in, what seemed like, glass boxes. There were microphones everywhere inside those boxes. Some of the boxes were bigger for entire bands and choirs to be in. Others were small just enough for one person. Outside of the glass boxes were several people in chairs running all sorts of gadgets and gizmos that I had never seen before.

Sarah and I were rather…stunned by all that we saw. "You two have never been in a recording studio before, have you?" Mr. Butters asked us, observing our awe and wonder of the place as he led us to an unoccupied room. We both answered simply by shaking our heads. "Well, this is it." Mr. Butters smiled as he waved his arms out to our glass box. Inside our box was a piano and two microphones. One was for the singer, the other was for the piano. Mr. Butters let us inside. At the piano was a tall, elderly man with a bright smile and a friendly face. He wore an old, wool suit and a worn, brown fedora. "That's Mr. Holt over there." Mr. Butters introduced. "Gene, these are our new singers."
"How do you do, youngsters?" Mr. Holt tipped his hat to us.
"Just fine, sir." I waved. "How are you?"
"Oh, mighty splendid, indeed, sir." Mr. Holt gave a big smile. "Mighty splendid."
"Good, good." Mr. Butters said anxiously. "We're all acquainted now."

Mr. Butters faced Sarah. "Now, little missy, are you ready to sing?"

Sarah seemed frightened to sing. She walked over to the singer's microphone before answering.

"So, I just sing in this microphone?" Sarah pointed at it. "That's it?"

"That's it." Mr. Butters smiled.

"Is he going to play while I sing?" Sarah pointed to Mr. Holt.

"Oh, no." Mr. Butters chuckled. "We may be efficient, but we're not *that* good. We don't have accompaniment for your song yet. If my boss likes your song, Mr. Holt will work on writing accompaniment for it. For now, you just ignore him and sing."

"I want Henry to sing with me." Sarah stated suddenly.

I raised my eyebrows. "I'm not that good."

Sarah eyed me. It almost looked like one of Scoefield's glares. Through the fire of her gaze, I could almost hear the words that her eyes were stating: "I am *NOT* singing alone."

"That's fine with me. You'll do great, son." Mr. Butters pushed me up to the microphone alongside Sarah.

Mr. Butters then left the room. We saw him appear behind the glass of the other room with another man and two men in chairs. The two men in chairs began hitting a bunch of switches and Mr. Butters gave a simple thumbs up to us. I blinked, feeling too nervous and ill prepared to start singing. Sarah, noticing that I wasn't singing, stayed silent as well. We just stood there as Mr. Holt, Mr. Butters, and the other three men behind the glass were all staring at us while the eerie silence continued.

Mr. Butters gave a worried smile to the man that stood next to him. The other man gave Mr. Butters a rather sour look. After some discussion, a very worried and sweaty Mr. Butters ran over to our room again.

"You kids need to sing. You remember the song, right?" He asked, tapping his foot.

"Yes." I nodded. "I'm sorry. We'll get it right this time."

"Please do." Mr. Butters said pleadingly. He hustled over to the other room.

"I'm scared." Sarah whispered to me as Mr. Butters once again gave the thumbs up.

I looked at her. Long and slowly, I gazed at her.

I wanted to help her. Just like I wanted to help her on that night I met her. I wanted to be strong for her.

So, I took her hand in mine. Sarah smiled, gently rubbing her thumb over my knuckles.

"Don't be." I whispered back. "You're the best singer in the world."

And we sang *Never*. We sang it like we sang it the first time. Strong. Filled with emotion.

Mr. Butters didn't look so worried anymore. The other man that was with him looked intrigued. Touched, even, by our song.

"I think that was a good test run." Mr. Butters told us as he was driving us home. "My boss thinks you two have got some talent and he doesn't say that often. Especially to kids. He thinks kids sound plum awful. I think he'll ask you to come back again."

"Well, you know where to find us, sir." I gave a small smile.

"Splendid! I'll keep in touch." Mr. Butters grinned. "You never know, your song might just be put on the radio someday! It should be rather exciting to hear it, wouldn't it?"

"We don't have a radio, sir."

"Really? Shame." Mr. Butters replied. "Remind me to get you a radio."

"Thank you." Sarah suddenly whispered to me. It was quiet enough that Mr. Butters didn't hear her.

"For what?" I whispered back.

Sarah's face was turning red, and she had a smile that was bigger than her face could hold. "For...everything you've done for me today. You're...a very sweet person, Henry." She was messing with her dress, not making eye-contact with me.

I leaned over and kissed her on the cheek. "You are far sweeter, Sarah."

Sarah looked dazed. Her face was redder and hotter than fire itself. "Henry..."

She couldn't hold it back, her smile was so radiant. She turned her face away, embarrassed of how much her emotions were showing on her face.

I smiled, probably blushing as well.

We didn't say anything for the rest of the ride home.

CHAPTER TEN

"So, where did we leave off?" I asked Sarah and Scoefield that night as I opened my Bible.

"Cain just killed his brother and fled from home." Sarah informed me, extremely excited that we were starting up our Bible stories again.

"Ah, yes." I nodded. "So, Adam and Eve, in a way, have now lost both of their sons. Abel is dead. Cain ran away. But God is truly merciful. It says in Genesis 4:25 – 26, 'And Adam knew his wife again; and she bare a son, and called his name Seth: For God, *said she,* hath appointed me another seed instead of Abel, whom Cain slew. And to Seth, to him also there was born a son; and he called his name Enos: then began men to call upon the name of the LORD'."

Then I stopped. I glanced at the next chapter.

"What is it?" Scoefield asked me.

"The next chapter is…well, it's about the generations of Adam. His son begat another son and that son begat another son. It's not the most interesting thing in the world."

"'Begat'?" Scoefield looked utterly confused.

"Well, then just tell us the summary of it." Sarah urged me.

"Well, basically, Adam had Seth, Seth had Enos, Enos had Cainan, Cainan had…Mahalaleel? (I think that's how you say it) Mahalaleel had Jared, Jared had Enoch, Enoch had Methuselah, Methuselah had Lamech, and Lamech had Noah."

"Strange names." Scoefield muttered. "They must've gotten picked on at school."

"The only school they would have had was home-school."
I chuckled. "So, I suppose their brothers could have picked on them, yes, but they probably had names that were just as peculiar."

"Home-school?" Scoefield raised his eyebrows. "That sounds too easy."

"You would be surprised." I mentioned. "Anyway, now we come to the life of Noah. A well-known and well-liked story of the Bible. It begins in chapter 6 of Genesis: 'And it came to pass, when men began to multiply on the face of the earth, and daughters were born unto them, That the sons of God saw the daughters of men that they *were* fair; and they took them wives of all which they chose. And the LORD said, My spirit shall not always strive with man, for that he also *is* flesh: yet his days shall be an hundred and twenty years. There were giants in the earth in those days; and also after that, when the sons of God came in unto the daughters of men, and they bare *children* to them, the same *became* mighty men which *were* of old, men of renown'."
I glanced up to make sure Scoefield and Sarah were keeping up.

"That seems like some random information thrown in there at the end." Sarah commented

"And more fairy-tale junk." Scoefield shook his head. "Explain it."

"Right." I said. "Well, by this time the earth was being filled with people. And men who knew God started becoming involved with women who didn't know God. They were getting married and having children."

"Because they were fair?" Sarah asked. "Like, fair in games?"

"Oh, no." I laughed. "Fair here means beautiful."

126

"Sounds like a good enough reason for me." Scoefield smiled. "The cavemen were lookin' around, saw girls and said 'She pretty. Want for wife!'."

"They weren't cavemen." I glowered at Scoefield.

"Well, if this happened like you said it did, it would'a happened back when dinosaurs were walkin' around and when people wore leopard underwear. So yeah. Cavemen." I stared at him for a second. "You do hear how they talk in the Bible, right? Remember how Cain spoke? 'Behold, thou hast driven me out this day from the face of the earth; and from thy face shall I be hid; and I shall be a fugitive and a vagabond in the earth;' Does that sound like caveman talk to you?"

Scoefield looked annoyed. "Whatever."

I continued. "So, men were chasing after women because of their looks rather than their integrity and relationship with God. And God is watching this, seeing their unwise and foolish choices. And God says that He is going to withdraw His Spirit from man. He would no longer strive with man, which means 'to rule'. God would no longer be able to rule among them because of man's fleshly lusts. God is, in essence, threatening to leave mankind to themselves. And we, left to ourselves, only race towards self-destruction."

Scoefield narrowed his eyes at me, as if I had just insulted him. But he said nothing.

"But what about men living to be a hundred and twenty years old?" Sarah questioned.

"Yeah, that's impossible." Scoefield spoke up. "Folks nowadays barely get to sixty before they kick the bucket."

127

"To tell you the truth, I'm not sure how people lived that long back then." I told them. "I mean, it says that Adam lived to be over nine-hundred years old."

Scoefield shook his head rapidly. "It ain't possible! Fairy-tale junk!"

Sarah simply gaped. "Nine-hundred?"

"Don't believe that, Sarah." Scoefield turned to her. "It ain't possible. The Bible's just filled with fantasy."

I was becoming rather discouraged at how Scoefield was taking this. Sarah looked at me, seeing if I would speak up against Scoefield's protests.

"*Help me, Father.*" I prayed silently.

"It's not fantasy." I said quietly. "It's truth."

"And how do ya' know that, Henry?" Scoefield countered. "You yourself said ya' don't know how someone could live to be a hundred and twenty. How do ya' know that Bible is truth?"

I swallowed. "Because the Holy Spirit within me tells me it is."

I looked at Sarah. "And the Holy Spirit within her tells her it is."

"Like you know what she feels about it." Scoefield looked angry. "Sarah doesn't believe in that junk."

"Yes, I do, Bradley." Sarah whispered.

Scoefield turned to her, surprised. "What?"

"It is true." Sarah nodded. "The Holy Spirit confirms it in my heart."

"Well, then why doesn't He confirm it in my heart?" Scoefield questioned fiercely. "Why am I the only one who sees this as baloney?"

Sarah and I looked at each other. Then back at him.

"Because, Scoefield…you are not saved." I told him gently. "The Holy Spirit isn't within you."

Scoefield was getting frustrated. "I don't need this. I don't want this. I've had enough of that Bible. I've had enough of these fairy-tales."

He stood up and grabbed his coat. "You two talk about 'em if ya' want. I won't be a part of this story time anymore."

"Where are you going, Bradley?" Sarah asked him, standing up.

"Out." Was all he said. Then he walked out the door and slammed it behind him.

"Why is this happening, Henry?" Sarah asked me, wiping tears from her face. "Why doesn't he just see that he needs God?"

"Some people just have hard hearts." I tried to console her. "God is working on him. I can definitely see that. He wouldn't be so defensive and angry if God wasn't nipping at his heart. But he's rejecting God every time it happens."

"How do we get him to see?" Sarah asked me. "There has to be some way."

I sighed. "Only God can do that. We have to pray for him. Pray that God opens his eyes."

Sarah sniffed. "I have been praying for him."

"Me too." I told her. "We just need to keep it up, I suppose."

"Yeah." Sarah nodded. "So, I guess our Bible group is now down to two people."

"It would seem that way." I replied.

"Well, we should finish Noah's story, huh?"

"Yes. Let's do that." I smiled for her.

I turned back to the passage where we left off. "'And GOD saw that the wickedness of man *was* great in the earth, and *that* every imagination of the thoughts of his heart *was* only evil continually. And it repented the LORD that He had made man on the earth, and it grieved Him at His heart. And the LORD said, I will destroy man whom I have created from the face of the earth; both man, and beast, and the creeping thing, and the fowls of the air; for it repenteth Me that I have made them'."

"Whoa, whoa." Sarah seemed startled. "God wanted to kill people?"

I shook my head. "Oh, no. God doesn't kill people because He wants to. Remember, God is holy. He cannot ignore wickedness. It must be brought to justice. Because the sons of God married the daughters of men, they raised children that only had one parent that knew God. But that parent was already compromising, so God was not being taught to the children. Eventually, God was being forgotten and people were just doing what they wanted to. They were imagining evil things and committing them. Murder. Rape. Incest. Sodomy. Vile sins. God had reached His limit with allowing those things to take place. Judgment was going to come to the earth."

Sarah seemed scared. "So...everyone died?"

I gave a small smile. "That's what you would think, until you read verse 8: 'But Noah found grace in the eyes of the LORD'."

Sarah gave a look of curiosity.

I continued. "'These *are* the generations of Noah: Noah was a just man *and* perfect in his generations, *and* Noah walked with God'."

130

I stopped there for a moment. "My father told me that this little verse says so much. It shows that God was looking at every single individual. Not just as a whole, or as a group. He was looking at the character, the integrity of every single man. And all were profusely wicked except for one. It also shows that Noah was quite exceptional. God declared the whole world as worthy of judgment, but Noah didn't go with what everyone else was doing. He remained faithful to God when no one else did. He and his family stood alone against the world. But God was with him."

"That would be so hard." Sarah said. "To stand alone against everybody."

"It is what we are called to, should it be necessary." I replied. "The world doesn't like Christians. Your brother won't be the only hostility that comes our way."

Sarah nodded. "I understand. Go on with the story."

I did so. "'And God said unto Noah, The end of all flesh is come before Me; for the earth is filled with violence through them; and, behold, I will destroy them with the earth. Make thee an ark of gopher wood; rooms shalt thou make in the ark, and shalt pitch it within and without with pitch'."

Sarah furrowed her brow in confusion. "An ark? Gopher wood? Pitch?"

"An ark...is like a boat." I tried to explain. "I mean, no one has ever really explained to me what the difference is between an ark and a boat."

"Why would Noah need a boat?" Sarah asked.

"Because of the flood."

"What flood?" She raised her eyebrows.

"Didn't I-?" I stuttered. I looked back at the Bible passage. "Oh! Silly me. I didn't tell you yet. God was going to destroy the world with a flood."

"A flood?"

"A great flood." I expounded. "One that would cover the entire earth."

Sarah widened her eyes. "That's a lot of water."

"Yes. So Noah really needed a boat."

"Yeah, but…" Sarah still looked confused. "If God flooded the whole world, where did the water go afterward? Did it just all dry up? And if it did, it probably took a long time. How much food were they able to get on that boat? I mean, you can only fit so much on a boat, and I'm sure he already had his family taking up a lot of the space."

I laughed. "Well, this wasn't your average boat. You're picturing something about the size of this room, yes?"

Sarah nodded.

"Now picture something four hundred and fifty feet long, seventy-five feet wide, and forty-five feet tall."

Sarah's mouth fell slightly open. "That's a big boat."

"Yes, it is." I chuckled.

"Why would they need something so huge?" Sarah wondered.

"Well, probably for living space, food storage, but mostly for the animals." I explained.

"Animals?"

"Oh yes, God wanted to save the animals too." I nodded. "Here, let's read what the Bible says about it. God is talking to Noah here: 'But with thee will I establish My covenant; and thou shalt come into the ark, thou, and thy sons, and thy wife, and thy sons' wives with thee. And of every living thing of all flesh, two of every *sort* shalt thou bring into the ark, to keep *them* alive with thee; they shall be male and female. Of fowls after their kind, and of cattle after their kind, of every creeping thing of the earth after his kind, two of every *sort* shall come unto thee, to keep *them* alive. And take thou unto thee of all food that is eaten, and thou shalt gather *it* to thee; and it shall be for food for thee, and for them. Thus did Noah; according to all that God commanded him, so did he'."

Sarah smiled pleasantly. "God saved all of the animals."
"You like that fact, huh?" I asked her.
"I do." She confirmed. "I like animals."
"Even snakes?" I grinned.
"Actually, yes." Sarah smiled even bigger. "I *do* like snakes. There one of my favorite animals."
"Really?" My grin was gone.
"Yes. I find them rather cute." She told me. "And interesting."
I was surprised. "Huh. Not many girls like snakes."
"Well, I'm not your average girl." Sarah threw back her hair. "I am Sarah Sunflower Scoefield."
"Sunflower?" I tried not to laugh. "Is that really your middle name?"
Sarah glared at me. "Don't laugh. Sunflowers are my favorite flowers."
"I'm not laughing." I wiped the smile off of my face.
"Uh-huh." Sarah eyed me. "So what happens after all the animals are on board the boat and everything?"
"It begins to rain." I told her, glad to be getting back on topic. "Rain for forty days and nights. A constant downpour four nine-hundred and sixty hours."
"All over the world?" Sarah questioned.

"All over the world." I confirmed. "It also says that the fountains of the great deep were broken up. My father told me that this meant water came shooting up from underground as well."

"Wow." Sarah marveled.

"And everything that wasn't on the ark died." I said solemnly.

Sarah sighed, looking troubled.

"Are you okay, Sarah?"

"Well...I don't understand something." She mentioned. "I know God is holy and that wickedness requires judgment, but Noah built that ark and didn't allow anyone to come aboard with him? I know that everyone was evil, but surely there were *some* people he knew and liked. Why wouldn't he tell them to...what's the word? Repent? Why wouldn't Noah tell them to repent and come on the ark with him?"

"He did." I replied.

"How do you know?"

"Well, 2 Peter 2:5 says 'And spared not the old world, but saved Noah the eighth *person*, a preacher of righteousness, bringing in the flood upon the world of the ungodly'. Noah was a preacher of righteousness. Preachers proclaim God's Word. He probably told everyone he could about the coming flood. They just didn't listen."

Sarah stared gravely at me. "They thought he was crazy, huh?"

"I assume so." I nodded. "Up to this point, it is believed that it had never rained before."

"No rain?" Sarah seemed surprised. "Then how did the plants get water?"

"Genesis 2:5 – 6 says 'And every plant of the field before it was in the earth, and every herb of the field before it grew:

for the LORD God had not caused it to rain upon the earth, and *there was* not a man to till the ground. But there went up a mist from the earth, and watered the whole face of the ground'."

"Incredible." Sarah said. "That's really strange to think that it didn't use to rain."

"Indeed." I concurred. "So, Noah telling everyone that it was going to rain must have been a big bite to chew. And not only rain, but so much that it would cover the entire earth."

"Yeah." Sarah suddenly squinted at me. "And you never answered some of my questions about that."

"Questions?"

"Where did all the water go after it flooded? Did it all dry up?"

"Oh, those questions." I chuckled. "Well, I don't think all of it dried up. You see, when God created the world, I think there was a canopy of water that surrounded the earth."

"A canopy of water?" Sarah gave a confused face.

"Yes." I assured her. "In Genesis 1:7, the Bible talks about waters under the firmament and waters above the firmament. 'Firmament' basically means the atmosphere. This water canopy is probably the water that would have fallen when the rain began."

"Okay, but what does that have to do with where all the water went?" Sarah questioned.

"It actually doesn't have much." I scratched my head with a grin. "It really just adds to the fact that the world was far different back then than it is now. That being said, I believe the earth had much less water on it back then than it does now."

"Why do you say that?"

"Just a personal opinion of mine, but there is some weight to it. After all, all of humanity gets drinking water from around 1% of water on the earth. 97% of all water on earth is salt-water. Can't use that. 2% of all water is glaciers. Too far away and it would take too long to melt and still be efficient. That leaves the final 1%. Fresh water rivers."

Sarah's confusion was rather obvious. "And why is that important to this topic?"

"Because humanity survives on 1% of the world's water. God orchestrated it that way. Why would He put all the extra water here if we didn't need it or even use it?"

"Because He does what He wants to?"

That made me laugh. "I suppose so, but I believe that He didn't originally put all that extra water here. I believe that the earth had significantly less water on it before the flood."

Sarah's eyes beamed with realization. "And after the flood, it simply all piled up together to make vast oceans."

I nodded. "Yes."

Sarah began thinking further. "You know, that would be nice if there wasn't so much water on earth. There would be more land to live on and it might have been easier to travel to nations across the seas."

"I guess we won't know." I concluded.

"Sad, but true." Sarah replied. "So, putting all that into perspective: that earth was far more land than sea, that it had never rained before, that Noah was saying there was going to be a worldwide flood…I can see now why they would think he was crazy."

"Many a man of God has been called crazy because of his faith in what God said." I agreed.

"So, they had a chance." Sarah said. "Noah warned them, they thought he was off his rocker, and when the flood came, it was too late."

"Unfortunately."

"Then, what happened with Noah and his family?" Sarah asked.

"They had to stay on the ark for quite some." I explained. "But eventually, the waters asswaged."

"Asswaged?"

"It's here in Genesis 8:1." I pointed in my Bible. "I think it means to settle or something of that nature."

"Oh. So the earth became what it is now and they lived the rest of their lives?"

"Yes." I smiled. "When they got off the ark, Noah built an altar to the Lord and offered up burnt offerings on it. And God, to show He would never again destroy the world with a great flood, put a rainbow in the sky."

"Oh, lovely." Sarah smiled. "Rainbows are a promise?"

"Mm-hmm." I smiled back. "So every time it rains, God still shows us that He won't send a worldwide flood."

"That's beautiful." Sarah beamed.

"Well, I suppose that's a good stopping point-" I began to close my Bible.

"Go on." Sarah urged me.

"What?" I blinked.

"Please, keep going." Sarah begged. "I want to hear more. I *need* to hear more. Until Bradley gets back."

I was surprised but further encouraged.

I opened my Bible again.

"Well, after the rainbow, there's not all that much except the generations of Noah. No need to go through that right now."

Sarah giggled as she lied down on her stomach, her hands under her chin. "More 'begat's?"

I laughed. "Yes, indeed."

"What about after that?"

I flipped through my Bible. "Ah. Well, after Noah and his children began repopulating the earth, we come to the story of Babel. In that time, there was no such thing as multiple languages. Genesis 11:1 says 'And the whole earth was of one language, and of one speech'."

"That would have made things easier." Sarah nodded. "No German language, no French, no Indian, just English."

I chuckled. "Now, now, it doesn't say that English was the only language. In fact, if my history is correct, English wasn't invented until around 1,000 A.D."

Sarah seemed disappointed. She pursed her lips together as if she had just tasted something sour. "Then what language did they speak?"

"The Bible doesn't say." I responded. "It may have been Hebrew or possibly Latin. I'm not certain."

"When were more languages invented?" Sarah perked up her eyebrows.

I put my finger to my lips. "Shh. We're getting to that."

"Then, by all means, O great Bible-reader, continue."

Sarah smiled a rather…alluring smile. I could hear it in her voice as well. A…smoother way of speaking. As if her words now had a different taste. Something that tasted like honey or chocolate. Then, to emphasize her flirtation, she winked at me.

I felt heat rushing to my face. *What on earth am I supposed to respond to **that** with?*

This rather flustered me. I felt excited and gooey, but also embarrassed and panicked.

So, I just did what she told me and continued with the story. I turned to my Bible and began to read.

"Anditcametopassastheyjourneyedfromtheeastthattheyfoun daplaininthelandofShinarandtheydweltthereAndtheysaidon etoanotherGotoletusmakebrickandburnthemthroughlyAndt heyhadbrickforstoneandslimehadtheyformorterAndtheysaid Gotoletusbuildusacityandatowerwhosetopmayreachuntohea venandletusmakeusanamelestwebescatteredabroaduponthef aceofthewholeearthAndtheLORDcamedowntoseethecityan dthetowerwhichthechildrenofmenbuildedAndtheLORDsaid Beholdthepeopleisoneandtheyhaveallonelanguageandthisth eybegintodoandnownothingwillberestrainedfromthemwhic htheyhaveimaginedtodoGotoletusgodownandthereconfoun dtheirlanguagethattheymaynotunderstandoneanother'sspee chSotheLORDscatteredthemabroadfromthenceuponthefacе ofalltheearthandtheyleftofftobuildthecityThereforeisthenam eofitcalledBabelbecausetheLORDdidthereconfoundthelang uageofalltheearthandfromthencedidtheLORDscatterthemab roaduponthefaceofalltheearth."

I spoke faster than I had ever done so before. What can I say? I was now both very nervous and fired up. Sarah responded in the only way she could:

Her eyes were wide, peering at me as to wonder if I was well or not. I, in turn, was starting to sweat because of how much of an imbecile I was sounding like.

Sarah took a deep breath as she sat up. "Henry, I've got no idea what you're sayin'."

I was suddenly startled at this new dialect Sarah displayed. "You just talked like Scoefield." I pointed out.

"And you just talked like a squirrel on espresso." Sarah laughed. "Of course I talk like my brother sometimes. We're around each other all the time. Now what was *that*?"

"Nothing. Nothing." I did my best to hide my embarrassment. "Back to the story."

I read it slow this time.

"Genesis 11:2 – 9. 'And it came to pass, as they journeyed from the east, that they found a plain in the land of Shinar; and they dwelt there. And they said one to another, Go to, let us make brick, and burn them throughly. And they had brick for stone, and slime had they for morter. And they said, Go to, let us build us a city and a tower, whose top *may reach* unto heaven; and let us make us a name, lest we be scattered abroad upon the face of the whole earth. And the LORD came down to see the city and the tower, which the children of men builded. And the LORD said, Behold, the people *is* one, and they have all one language; and this they begin to do: and now nothing will be restrained from them, which they have imagined to do. Go to, let Us go down, and there confound their language, that they may not understand one another's speech. So the LORD scattered them abroad from thence upon the face of all the earth: and they left off to build the city. Therefore is the name of it called Babel; because the LORD did there confound the language of all the earth: and from thence did the LORD scatter them abroad upon the face of all the earth'."

"That's much better." Sarah was still trying to hold in laughter. "Now, please explain."

I nodded as I put my face further into my Bible, trying to avoid her gaze.

"Well, you see, these men almost sound spiritual, right?" I asked her.

Sarah placed her hand on my Bible and gently pulled it away from my face. My eyes met hers once again. Her dancing, shimmering, warm eyes.

140

"Yes, they do." She spoke softly as her smile continued to melt me. She didn't even have to say it for me to hear it. I could see it in her eyes, her smile, her body language, even hear it in the song that was her voice:

"Don't hide from me."

And I obeyed. I set the Bible back in my lap.

I cleared my throat. "Well, er, yes, it may sound spiritual with the whole 'let us build us a city and a tower, whose top *may reach* unto heaven'. The thing is that they weren't doing that to get closer to God. They were doing that so they could 'worship' the sun, moon, and stars."

"Their god was the sun, moon, and stars?" Sarah brought up. "That sounds rather silly."

"Well, the funny thing is that no matter what you believe about life, or God, or how we got here, or where we are going, every man and woman has a god. Every man and woman will worship something. Whether it be the one, true God, or something lesser."

"Give me an example." Sarah told me.

"Well, okay." I folded my arms together as I thought. "… Hmm. Well, my grandfather actually had his god in his money."

Sarah didn't say anything to that. She just looked at me with a face that just seemed to say "Tell me more".

I continued. "My grandfather was a rich man and he loved being rich. But when the depression came along, it hit Grandfather hard. He lost all of his money and it caused him to have a heart attack. He died before we could reach the hospital."

"I'm very sorry, Henry." Sarah looked at me with sad eyes.

"Thank you." Was all I said for a while. Then I cleared my throat. "That's one example, anyway. A person could make

141

anything his or her god: their career, family, materials, pleasure, food, a relationship, themselves. The list is enormous."

"That's really sad." Sarah echoed. "That people would make things that can do nothing for you the most important thing in their life."

"It is. And the people at Babel made creation their god." I got back to the Bible. "And, as you know, God is holy. Worshipping the sun, moon, and stars is sinful because God deserves all the worship. Creation has no consciousness to even appreciate the worship man could give it. It's not only sinful but it's useless and vain. But God is holy and must bring righteous judgment to those who are ripe for it."

"So, confornding their language was the judgment God gave?" Sarah questioned. "That seems a little light for judgment."

"Confounding it, yes." I couldn't help but snicker.

"You're making fun of me." Sarah narrowed her eyes.

"If you look at this passage, however, God was actually targeting their greatest desire." I noted, avoiding the fact that I had been making fun of her. Sarah was a good sport about it and let it go.

"Which is?" She pondered.

"They built Babel to make a name for themselves, so they wouldn't be scattered across the earth from each other." I explained. "God swooped in, *confounded* their language, and they were forced to separate from each other."

Sarah caught how I emphasized 'confounded'. She didn't humor me though. She acted as if I hadn't said anything. I was a little disappointed. Egging her on was fun.

"So, if we refuse to listen to God, sometimes He'll go after the thing we want the most." Sarah observed.

"Yes." I concurred. "It's how He gets our attention. And this isn't the only place in the Bible where God does that."

"I didn't think so." Sarah answered. "People like to chase after things with all of their heart. In an unhealthy way. In a wrong way. I've seen that many times just in my own life."

"It's a common thing to see." I agreed. I then glanced at my Bible. "So, do you want to keep going or stop here?"

Sarah looked at me with her big green eyes. "Let's keep going until Bradley gets back, please."

I sighed with a smile. I turned the page in my Bible. "Okay. Oh, well here it talks of more 'begats'. Let me just flip past those. Ah. Here we are. Next, we come to Abraham."

Sarah's eyes got huge. "Abraham Lincoln is in the Bible?"

I did my best to hold in my laughter. I didn't do such a good job.

"That would be quite a wonderful thing, I suppose." I said in response. "But no, this is a different Abraham. And, where we are at in the Bible, that's actually not even his name yet. His name, for now, is Abram."

Sarah waited eagerly for me to begin this new Bible story. She sat cross-legged with a giddy fire in her eyes. "Abram was the son of a man named Terah. Terah had three sons: Abram, Nahor, and Haran. And, in the natural course of life, they all obtained wives. However, Haran died soon after his son, Lot, was born. And, to add to the unfortunate event, Abram's wife, Sarai, could not bear children."

In Sarah's eyes, I saw a horrible sense of sorrow. I could tell she understood the fervent desire to be able to bear children. It must be quite a horror for women to discover they cannot have their own children.

I could see so much about this Sarah Scoefield…just in her eyes. It is wonderful and curious how the eyes are somehow linked to the heart.

"And that's when God came to Abram." I smiled. "Genesis 12:1 – 3 says 'Now the LORD had said unto Abram, Get thee out of thy country, and from thy kindred, and from thy father's house, unto a land that I will shew thee: And I will make of thee a great nation, and I will bless thee, and make thy name great; and thou shalt be a blessing: And I will bless them that bless thee, and curse him that curseth thee: and in thee shall all families of the earth be blessed'."

"Wow, that was nice of God." Sarah remarked. "Well, except for the part about leaving his family behind."

"It was probably hard for Abram to do that." I nodded. "In that culture, families usually lived together for their whole lives."

"But he obeyed God, right?"

I grinned. "If he didn't, this would've been a very short story, huh?"

Sarah smiled pleasantly at that. "Keep reading."

"'So Abram departed, as the LORD had spoken unto him; and Lot went with him: and Abram *was* seventy and five years old when he-'"

"Seventy-five?" Sarah marveled. "That's a little old to be traveling, isn't it? He should be in a nursing home."

"Probably." I agreed. "I've never heard of anyone in our time living over sixty-five."

"My grandpa Leppy lived until he was eighty." Sarah mentioned. "He had my mom later in life. I think he was forty when she was born. Grandpa Leppy died not long before she did."

I took that in. Her grandfather dying right before her parents did. The same thing happened with me. How alike our situation truly was. But what could I say? 'I'm sorry'? 'That is very sad'?

"Was he saved?" Is what really came out of my mouth.

"I don't know." Sarah admitted, staring at the wall. "Pop didn't like him, so we didn't see him much. But he did go to church. And when we were with him, he would talk about the Bible. But I can't say if he was saved or not. I hope so. I think so. But I'm not for sure."

"Well, if he was saved, you'll see him again." I gave a small smile.

She returned the smile back to me. "Sorry for getting off on that rabbit trail."

"It's fine." I told her. "Shall I resume?"

"Please do."

I turned back to my Bible. "'And Abram *was* seventy and five years old when he departed out of Haran. And Abram took Sarai his wife, and Lot his brother's son, and all their substance that they had gathered, and the souls that they had gotten in Haran; and they went forth to go into the land of Canaan; and into the land of Canaan they came. And Abram passed through the land unto the place of Sichem, unto the plain of Moreh. And the Canaanite *was* then in the land. And the LORD appeared unto Abram, and said, Unto thy seed will I give this land: and there builded he an altar unto the LORD, who appeared unto him. And he removed from thence unto a mountain on the east of Bethel, and pitched his tent, *having* Bethel on the west, and Hai on the east: and there he builded an altar unto the LORD, and called upon the name of the LORD'."

Sarah suddenly raised her hand.

145

"Yes?"

"Why did God give Abram the land?" Sarah put her hand down. "What was so special about him?"

"I can't say." I confessed. "But I know that God has a unique plan for each and every person. He has a plan for you and me. God has chosen us for something just as He chose Abram for something. Who knows? It could be just as grand."

Sarah thought on that, but said nothing.

I continued. "'And Abram journeyed, going on still toward the south. And there was a famine in the land: and Abram went down into Egypt to sojourn there; for the famine *was* grievous in the land. And it came to pass, when he was come near to enter into Egypt, that he said unto Sarai his wife, Behold now, I know that thou *art* a fair woman to look upon: Therefore it shall come to pass, when the Egyptians shall see thee, that they shall say, This *is* his wife: and they will kill me, but they will save thee alive'."

"A famine is when there isn't any food, right?" Sarah asked me.

"That's right." I responded.

"Okay." Sarah began thinking out loud. She placed her hand to her chin as to look like she was thinking. Her eyes drifted upward to look at the ceiling. "So, there's a famine. They need food. They go down to Egypt to get food, but Abram is worried that the Egyptians will kill him for his drop-dead gorgeous wife..."

Sarah suddenly broke out of her thinking pose to look right at me. An expression of utter disgust was all over her face. "Don't tell me that Abram married a woman that was fifty years younger than he was."

"He didn't." I reassured her with a laughing smile. "She was just ten years younger than he was."

Sarah's eyes widened. "You're telling me this dame was sixty-five and yet was still the bee's knees?"

I blinked. "Well, that was very American."

"She's sixty-five and yet still so beautiful that everyone wants her." Sarah explained.

"It would seem so." I mentioned.

"That can't be true." Sarah narrowed her eyes.

"You'll see in just a jiffy." I said. "Okay, so Abram says to Sarai 'Say, I pray thee, thou *art* my sister: that it may be well with me for thy sake; and my soul shall live because of thee'."

"He's a bit of a worry-wart, isn't he?" Sarah piped up. "I mean, calling his wife his sister? That's so peculiar."

"Just wait until I finish." I told her. "It will make sense then. 'And it came to pass, that, when Abram was come into Egypt, the Egyptians beheld the woman that she *was* very fair-'"

"No way." Sarah's eyes got wide again. "They actually thought she was beautiful?"

"The Bible says she was." I answered.

"She's sixty-five!" Sarah argued. "How many old women do you see nowadays and think 'dang! She's good looking!'?"

"There is only one woman I think about that is truly beautiful." I said quietly as I gave a tiny smile. "And she's almost seventeen."

Sarah's cheeks immediately burned bright red as she sat up straight. I reckon that I had surprised her with that. She knew that I was talking about her.

Sarah's eyes were all over the room, her mouth trying to stutter words together but failing. "That's-…I'm not…You-You don't really-…I can't-…You-…Just trying-…" Suddenly, she just dropped her head and sighed heavily. "Let's just continue the story, please."

I was strangely amused by her reaction. Not the fact that I had made her embarrass herself, but the fact that I could ruffle her so. To me, it felt like a good sign. But I didn't push her. I kept reading. "'The princes also of Pharaoh saw her, and commended her before Pharaoh: and the woman was taken into Pharaoh's house. And he entreated Abram well for her sake: and he had sheep, and oxen, and he asses, and menservants, and maidservants, and she asses, and camels. And the LORD plagued Pharaoh and his house with great plagues because of Sarai Abram's wife. And Pharaoh called Abram, and said, What *is* this *that* thou hast done unto me? why didst thou not tell me that she *was* thy wife? Why saidst thou, She *is* my sister? so I might have taken her to me to wife: now therefore behold thy wife, take *her*, and go thy way. And Pharaoh commanded *his* men concerning him: and they sent him away, and his wife, and all that he had'."

I looked up from my Bible. Sarah was looking at the floor, her face redder than ever.
"What's this?" I asked in a playful tone. "She who was asking questions left and right tonight is now silenced?"
"Meh." Sarah muttered, still staring at the ground.
I chuckled to myself, but I didn't press further. "Come on, I know you have questions."

Sarah gazed up at me with an adamant fierce look. Almost angry-looking, but there was a confident smile shining on her face.

"As a matter of fact, Henry Engel, I have no questions for you. I understand this passage perfectly. I do not need your explanation whatsoever. Pharaoh took Abram's wife to be his own, for she was beautiful. Abram wasn't going to say anything because he was afraid for his life. But, of course, God has a plan for Abram and Sarai. And though Abram's cowardice allowed Sarai to be taken, God would not let her be anyone but Abram's. He plagued Pharaoh to get his attention. Once God has Pharaoh's attention, He either told Pharaoh Himself that Sarai was Abram's wife, or Sarai told him. Being less than a scoundrel, Pharaoh returned to Abram she that was rightly his and sent them away."

I was taken aback. "That was quite insightful."

Sarah raised her eyebrows with a scoff hiding behind her eyes. "What? Women can't be insightful?"

"I didn't say that." I was growing nervous.

"Oh, so *I* can't be insightful? Is that what you're saying?" Sarah's eyes hardened.

Terror struck at my feeble heart. What is a man to do when a woman reads things in his words that weren't there? Just moments ago, I was getting a swelled head over my ability to affect her emotions. Now, my arrogance had back-fired, pushing me to be careless with my words.

"*Pride goeth before destruction, and an haughty spirit before a fall.*" I quoted Proverbs 16:18 in my head.

"I didn't mean that." I scrambled with my words. "I-I-I was just saying-I was meaning that-"

I was stopped by a cruel smile that was working its way across Sarah's face.

"I got you." Sarah winked. "I got you good."

"What?"

"I wasn't serious, Henry." Sarah batted her eyes at me. "I just wanted to get you back."

I blinked, putting together what she was saying. "…Oh. Well…yes, you were right about the passage."

"But there's more you want to say." Sarah smiled. "More you'd like to add."

"No, I-"

"Henry." Sarah stopped me.

I looked at her.

"I know you." Her smile shined brightly. "Tell me."

I sighed, feeling both warm inside and on my face. "Well, I find it interesting that Pharaoh here gave all those gifts to Abram: sheep, oxen, donkeys, camels, and servants, both men and women. He gives him all that, then Pharaoh discovers that Sarai is Abram's wife, and gives her back. There is no evidence here that Pharaoh was ever returned those gifts after he returned Sarai. So, Pharaoh simply received nothing in that entire adventure. In fact, he lost things."

"That's a real bummer." Sarah agreed. "But he was **Pharaoh**. I mean, being the king of Egypt, you aren't exactly in wanting."

"That's very true." I nodded to her. "And it's funny you should say that, because guess what problems Abram has next."

"What?" Sarah's eyes got wide with anticipation.

"He had too much stuff." I smiled.

"How is that even possible?" Sarah gawked. "Read it to me."

I obeyed. "'And Abram went up out of Egypt, he, and his wife, and all that he had, and Lot with him, into the south. And Abram *was* very rich in cattle, in silver, and in gold. And he went on his journeys from the south even to Bethel, unto the place where his tent had been at the beginning, between Bethel and Hai; Unto the place of the altar, which he had made there at the first: and there Abram called on the name of the LORD. And Lot also, which went with Abram, had flocks, and herds, and tents. And the land was not able to bear them, that they might dwell together: for their substance was great, so that they could not dwell together. And there was a strife between the herdmen of Abram's cattle and the herdmen of Lot's cattle: and the Canaanite and the Perizzite dwelled then in the land'.'"
Sarah could not fathom it. "They had so much stuff that they couldn't live together? That's just bonkers!"
"I know, but that's apparently the case." I replied. "They did come up with a solution, however."
"Oh?"
"'And Abram said unto Lot, Let there be no strife, I pray thee, between me and thee, and between my herdmen and thy herdmen; for we *be* brethren. *Is* not the whole land before thee? separate thyself, I pray thee, from me: if *thou wilt take* the left hand, then I will go to the right; or if *thou depart* to the right hand, then I will go to the left. And Lot lifted up his eyes, and beheld all the plain of Jordan, that it *was* well watered every where, before the LORD destroyed Sodom and Gomorrah, *even* as the garden of the LORD, like the land of Egypt, as thou comest unto Zoar. Then Lot chose him all the plain of Jordan; and Lot journeyed east: and they separated themselves the one from the other'.'"
Sarah's face immediately turned crestfallen. "Separate? They separated?"

I paused as I watched Sarah's gaze fell towards the floor. Her arms, in a slow motion, wrapped around her middle-section. It was almost like she was giving herself a hug.

"Family should never separate because of things." She whispered softly. "Family should never separate at all, actually. They should have found another way. If they had too much stuff, they could have gotten rid of it. You don't need to be rich if it's causing problems. I mean, look at us..."

Sarah slowly trailed off, her eyes staring off into some unknown land. Possibly a memory. I myself took some time at that instant to reflect on the passage. What if I had been in that situation? Would I choose as Abram did? I liked to have thought that I wouldn't have, but how could I say whether or not I would do something? I don't know the end of my story. And if I had, I would have done things differently. But I didn't know, so I did things that I now regret.

I sighed as I shook myself out of my deep thoughts. I looked back at Sarah. How sad she looked. How radiant and sad. At that moment, I felt somewhat dismal. Sarah was sad because Abram and Lot separated. The consequences of that decision were far more depressing, but she didn't know that yet. I knew what was coming. She didn't. I glanced down at my Bible and read the next couple of verses silently to myself. 'Abram dwelled in the land of Canaan, and Lot dwelled in the cities of the plain, and pitched *his* tent toward Sodom. But the men of Sodom *were* wicked and sinners before the LORD exceedingly.' I sighed again and closed my Bible.

"That's a good place to stop." I spoke to Sarah.

Sarah glanced up at me. It was at that moment that I believe Sarah and I both suddenly realized how utterly fatigued we were. Who knew what the time was? Sarah's eyes seemed to droop as her face also seemed to sag. I'm sure mine was similar, if not identical. We had been up much longer than we thought we would.

"Bed?" Sarah questioned me.

I nodded. "Bed."

As we prepared for sleep, I was troubled at the fact that Scoefield was not back yet. We had probably been up for an extra hour, maybe more. Where was Scoefield?

As Sarah and I settled in the bed alone, I couldn't help but enjoy not having her brother between us. Sarah quickly lulled off to sleep. Before I joined her, I reached out and took her hand.

CHAPTER ELEVEN

"You were gone pretty long last night." I mentioned to Scoefield on our walk back from the malt shop. It was the next day. The next evening, actually. To be honest, nothing much happened that day that was exceptional. Well, except waking up in the morning. I thought I was hugging Sarah in my sleep, but being lightly pushed away by her every now and again. When I awoke, I realized, to my horror, that I was hugging Scoefield and was constantly being shoved off by him.

Awkward.

But later that day, God had provided me with thirty cents yet again and Scoefield and I went to the malt shop, as per the usual. We were carrying back our weekly soda pops when our conversation struck up.

"Maybe I wanted to be alone for a while." Scoefield said to me.

I was concerned for my friend. Scoefield hadn't come back to the shack until very late, almost very early, that morning. "You fought someone?" I poked.

Scoefield chuckled, unimpressed. "No."

"What happened, then?" I asked, worried.

Scoefield gave me an exasperated glare. "What are ya'? My mama?"

"I just worry about you." I defended.

"Well…" Scoefield rubbed his nose. "I don't need ya' to worry about me."

"Why not?" I stopped walking, staring at him adamantly.

"You worry about your sister, right? Why can't I worry about my brother?"

Scoefield stopped, his entire countenance softening.
"Brother? Henry, what're-"
"I know you don't like hearing the Bible, but it says that
'there is a friend that sticketh closer than a brother'.
Scoefield, I have no family anymore. I want you and Sarah
to be my family now. You are like a brother to me."

That was bold of me. I am usually not so bold. I
suppose Scoefield had been rubbing off on me. But, I could
also see, in Scoefield's eyes, surprise. At the time, I wasn't
sure if it was good surprise or bad. Perhaps it was neutral, I
had thought.
A long pause echoed between us as Scoefield shook his
head, scratched his neck and looked me in the eye.
"Henry...I'm not your brother. Okay? I *am* your friend.
But I am not your brother. Stop worryin' about me. Got it?"
He then turned and continued walking. For a moment, I
found myself burning red with embarrassment. How lofty I
had been to assume that Scoefield would see me as a
brother. A friend was good, but it was far from brother.

I sighed to myself as Scoefield pulled further and
further out of view. An overwhelming amount of emotions
swirled within me: depression, regret, disappointment...
basically all the feelings that could be associated with
'sad'.
Again, I know that this sounds really 'boo-hoo'ey of me.
My friend wasn't as close as I imagined him to be. So
what? What's the big deal? People might ask me that. And
you know what? I can't say that it is something worth
crying over (Let it be known, however, that I did *not* cry
over this issue. No tears were shed). But everyone has
different complications in their life. Something that is

155

hurtful to one person may roll off the shoulders of another. No two people are identical. So, I suppose, the hidden moral in what I am trying to say is simply this: understand people. Wow, that was vague, wasn't it? Okay, how about this...Don't think that just because something works with one person that it will automatically work with another. And that could be anything. Criticism, rebuke, encouragement, joking, preaching, instruction, hugging, pets, books, plants, radios, ice cream...I'm getting a little off topic. You get the idea, right? The basic point of all of this ranting, really, is that Scoefield and I were beginning to drift apart. At least, that was evident to me. Every night when Sarah and I were going to have our Bible time, Scoefield would leave. And he would never tell us where he went during those times. I worried about him. I prayed for him. But what else could I do?

Instead, I focused on Sarah...Which wasn't exactly the best of ideas. But I'm getting ahead of myself. Let's get back to the story.

"Now, I have something unfortunate news about what happens next." I began while opening my Bible. Sarah furrowed her eyebrows, looking uneasily sad. She waited nervously as I glanced through the passage.

"Abram's and Lot's decision to separate led to further consequences." I explained. "Lot went to live in the city of Sodom."

"Sodom?"

"Sodom." I confirmed gravely. "The Bible calls it a city full of men who were 'wicked and sinners before the Lord exceedingly'."

Sarah gave a slightly confused face. "But aren't we all sinners?"

156

"Yes." I told her. "But I think this verse points more to that they were 'sinners before the Lord'. As in, they were declaring their sin openly in front of everyone and not caring about it. They were proud of their sin."

"Not good." Sarah mumbled.

"No. And Lot went to live there."

Sarah slumped. "Even worse."

"But we'll get back to that later." I flipped through some pages. "For now, we get back to Abram."

Sarah's mouth dropped open with an 'are you kidding me?' expression. "You're going to tell me that Lot went to live there in a wicked city full of evil men and then just skip back over to Abram?"

"It's what the Bible does." I laughed inwardly at her reaction.

"That's just torture!" Sarah gaped.

"Shh." I shushed with a grin. "Let's get back to the Bible." Sarah's eyes had mini daggers in them, but she said nothing. She simply folded her arms and 'humph'ed. I did my best to contain my smile as I quickly skimmed over the next verses. "So, you remember when I told you that God promised He would give Abram a land that He would show him?"

Sarah nodded, her expression softening.

"This is when that happens." I told her. "God tells Abram to look west, east, south, and north. God tells Abram that everything he sees will be his land, and that God will give it to Abram's descendants as well."

"Wow." Sarah marveled. "Everything he could see?"

I nodded. "But then we come to Chedolaomer."

"Kay-doe-lay-o-mur?" Sarah tried. "Sounds like a villain name."

157

"You're not too far off." I responded. "And he's not the only one, actually. He just seems to be the leader of all of them."

"Them?"

"Kings." I clarified. "Kings of the land. Amraphel, Arioch, Tidal, and Chedolaomer. Apparently, Chedolaomer had the cities of Sodom and Gomorrah under his reign. They served him for twelve years, but they rebelled against him in the thirteenth year."

"Oh no." Sarah drew in a sharp breath. I could see how much she was getting into the story. Of course, it was a true account, but I really liked how much Sarah was being drawn in. It was getting me rather excited as well, so I did my best to add the necessary theatrics to it.

"So Chedolaomer came for blood." I whispered darkly, in the most masculine voice I could muster.

"But Lot lives there!" Sarah shrieked. "Don't tell me he died!"

"They came and conquered." I continued, keeping within character. "Like a rampaging beast, Chedolaomer was an unstoppable force. What defenses Sodom and Gomorrah could assemble fell powerlessly against Chedolaomer's might. He pillaged Sodom and Gomorrah of their goods… and their people."

Sarah had managed to snatch her coat and held it in her arms, to have something she could squeeze if she became over-anxious. By this time, she was strangling it.

"Lot was taken captive." I ended her torment. "Along with many other inhabitants."

"He lived!" Sarah gasped in relief. Then she paused. "As… a prisoner?"

158

"Yes. But God always watches out for those who are His."
I smiled. "A man escaped and told Abram."

Sarah seemed skeptic. "What could Abram do? He was just one guy. One very old guy."

"One very old, very *wealthy* guy." I added. "He had servants."

"People that served him tea, great." Sarah's skepticism was unchallenged.

"May I ask you something?" I suddenly changed key.

Sarah seemed a bit surprised at my question. "Um, yes?"

"Why am I here?"

Sarah narrowed her eyes at me. "…I'm confused at the question. Be more specific."

"What is my purpose to be here with you, Sarah Scoefield?" I clarified.

"You're to look after me."

"Protect you?"

"Yes."

"And, in return, I am given a place to sleep and food to eat." I noted.

"Yes…" Sarah seemed to know I was onto something, but didn't quite figure it out just yet.

"Your brother employed me, so to speak, to act as a guard for you." I replied. "You don't think Abram could have done the same?"

"So…Abram's servants were trained to be guards?" Sarah put it together. "Soldiers?"

I nodded. "Abram was rich and he was old. Thieves target those exact people because they have money, yet they are feeble. He would need protection over his family. And not just Sarah. But Lot was his family too."

"You don't mean…" Sarah gasped.

I read it directly from the Bible. "'And when Abram heard that his brother was taken captive, he armed his trained *servants*, born in his own house, three hundred and eighteen, and pursued *them* unto Dan'."

"Ooo." Sarah smiled. "But can Abram and three hundred men take down Cheedo-lame-er?"

"That is a very valid question." I confessed, ignoring Sarah's mispronunciation. "The odds were against them: Though Abram and his servants had been trained in the art of war, they were mainly farmers and shepherds. And the enemy they were going up against? Abram's servants added up to three hundred some, while they most likely had at least one thousand some. And this was an army that just had come from victory, not defeat. These were hardened, bloody, triumphant men of war."

Sarah was becoming concerned.

"But with age comes experience." I added. "Abram divided his men around the enemy camp. He was going to attack from several different quarters, so as to appear more numerous in men. He attacked at night, so as to catch them off guard. These men were probably either celebrating or sleeping, then suddenly – POW! Swords are slashing, clanging, swooshing! War is everywhere! Who is ally? Who is enemy? Such surprise would have made Chedolaomer's forces panic, possibly even to the point where they started attacking their own troops. But, eventually, Chedolaomer's forces fled. They were unprepared and overcome. And, the Bible doesn't suggest that Abram lost any of his men."

"None of his men died?" Sarah raised her eyebrows. "And they completely wiped out Chedolaomer?"

"Hey, you got it right this time." I pointed out.

Sarah smiled victoriously. "It just took me a couple times. So, they beat him completely?"

"The Bible says 'And he brought back all the goods, and also brought again his brother Lot, and his goods, and the women also, and the people', so I'm not sure whether or not Abram actually destroyed all of them or just ran them off. He could have done either, but the point was rescuing Lot."

I kept gazing at the word 'brother' in verse 16 of chapter 14.

"So, why did he save everyone if most of those people were very wicked?" Sarah pondered. "Why not just get Lot?"

"Just because someone is wicked doesn't mean you can't care for them." I pointed out. "After all, we all were lost and without God at one point. Helping others who are without God may be the first step to them getting saved." Sarah smiled and nodded in comprehension.

"So, after this, there is a rather random encounter with a man known as Melchizedek." I continued.

Sarah sighed. "What is it with all these guys with complicated names?"

"He's a curious character, Melchizedek." I kept going, skimming my Bible. "He is called the king of Salem and the priest of the most high God. But no one, that I know of, is entirely sure who this guy really is. Some people think that he is Shem, the son of Noah. But let's be honest, that's a ridiculous theory. Others tend to believe that he is Jesus."

That got Sarah's attention. "What? Jesus? That can't be right. He was born in the New Testament, wasn't He?"

"Yes." I acknowledged. "But Jesus is God, and God has always been. Therefore, Jesus has always been. If

161

Melchizedek was Jesus, He would be a preincarnate Christ."

"Preincarnate?"

"Existing before birth." I told her. "It's confusing."

"You're telling me." Sarah looked utterly befuddled.

"Regardless of who Melchizedek is, he came to bless Abram." I began to read from the passage. "'And he blessed him, and said, Blessed *be* Abram of the most high God, possessor of heaven and earth: And blessed be the most high God, which hath delivered thine enemies into thy hand. And he gave him tithes of all'."

"Wait." Sarah stopped me. "When it says 'he gave him tithes of all', is it saying Abram gave Melchizo-whatever tithes or the other way around? Tithe is what we give at church, right?"

I paused. "I believe it is Abram that gave tithes to Melchizedek. It wouldn't exactly make sense the other way around. Melchizedek was the priest of God. And tithe is a tenth of what we earn and we give it back to God, yes. However, here, it says that Abram gave tithes of all. Of all that he had, he gave a tenth of it."

"That's impressive." Sarah replied. "He had tons of stuff and he gave a tenth of all of it."

Sarah then paused in thought for a moment. "He was quite the godly man. Even when he was rich, he was still willing to give up the amount that God asked for."

"Yes." I smiled. "It was all God's anyway. He owns everything we have here on this world. Abram knew that God had given him all he had, so he gave back ten percent of it."

I chuckled a bit as I glanced at the next verses. "And it's funny, because right after Abram gives back to God, Satan throws temptation at him. The king of Sodom comes to Abram and says to him 'Give me the persons, and take the goods to thyself'."

"Why is that temptation?" Sarah asked. "Wouldn't be perfectly fine if Abram took all of the-what do you call it? ...Spoils?"

"Abram had his reasons." I explained. "Here, listen to this: 'And Abram said to the king of Sodom, I have lift up mine hand unto the LORD, the most high God, the possessor of heaven and earth, That I will not *take* from a thread even to a shoelatchet, and that I will not take any thing that *is* thine, lest thou shouldest say, I have made Abram rich'."

"So he made a vow." Sarah concluded. "And he didn't want people saying that the king of Sodom made him rich."

"Exactly." I agreed. "God was the one who was providing for Abram and he wanted everyone to know that it was Him rather than anyone else."

"Very wise." Sarah complimented. "What happens next?"

I was reading the next chapter as she asked this. "You know...I think I would rather just read this to you then say it."

"Okay." Sarah said.

I began. "'After these things the word of the LORD came unto Abram in a vision, saying, Fear not, Abram: I *am* thy shield, *and* thy exceeding great reward. And Abram said, Lord GOD, what wilt Thou give me, seeing I go childless, and the steward of my house *is* this Eliezer of Damascus? And Abram said, Behold, to me Thou hast given no seed: and, lo, one born in my house is mine heir. And, behold, the word of the LORD *came* unto him, saying, This shall not be thine heir; but he that shall come forth out of thine own bowels shall be thine heir. And He

163

brought him forth abroad, and said, Look now toward heaven, and tell the stars, if thou be able to number them: and He said unto him, So shall thy seed be. And he believed in the LORD; and He counted it to him for righteousness. And He said unto him, I *am* the LORD that brought thee out of Ur of the Chaldees, to give thee this land to inherit it. And he said, Lord GOD, whereby shall I know that I shall inherit it? And He said unto him, Take me an heifer of three years old, and a she goat of three years old, and a ram of three years old, and a turtledove, and a young pigeon. And he took unto him all these, and divided them in the midst, and laid each piece one against another: but the birds divided he not. And when the fowls came down upon the carcases, Abram drove them away. And when the sun was going down, a deep sleep fell upon Abram; and, lo, an horror of great darkness fell upon him'."

"Golly." Sarah said. "What does it all mean?"
"Well, in order to become a great nation as God told him he would, Abram would have to have a child." I told her. "Seeing that he and Sarai were childless, this posed a problem. But God told Abram that he would have a son. And Abram, against all earthly knowledge, believed God. He had no logical reason to believe that he would have a son, but he believed God anyway, and God esteemed it worthy of righteousness. God again promised Abram a great people would come from his seed and they would inhabit the land that Abram walked on."
"But what about the offering Abram was preparing?" Sarah questioned. "Dividing the carcasses? The deep sleep? 'Horror of great darkness'?"

I read through my Bible. "Here, let me read you this part and then I will explain. 'And it came to pass, that, when the sun went down, and it was dark, behold a smoking furnace, and a burning lamp that passed between those pieces. In the same day the LORD made a covenant with Abram, saying, Unto thy seed have I given this land, from the river of Egypt unto the great river, the river Euphrates: The Kenites, and the Kenizzites, and the Kadmonites, And the Hittites, and the Perizzites, and the Rephaims, And the Amorites, and the Canaanites, and the Girgashites, and the Jebusites'."

I scratched my chin as I chose my words carefully. "God made a very special covenant with Abram that day. I believe it is known as the Abrahamic Covenant. It was also a blood covenant. A very serious vow. You see, in those times, if two people were making a very serious vow between the two of them, they would make a blood covenant. They would gather up the animals seen in this passage, tear them in two pieces, and walk between the carcasses."

Sarah looked horrified. "Why?"

"It was to say 'If I break my side of the oath, let this be done to me'." I expounded.

"So, if one broke the vow, they would be killed?"

"Yes." I said gravely. "Death was the punishment of breaking the blood covenant. And God was showing Abram that He was going to do what He said He would. He was going to give Abram an heir. He was going to give Abram's descendants the land of Israel."

"We have an issue, though." Sarah spoke.

"What's that?"

"Abram didn't walk between the bodies." Sarah pointed out. "He was in a deep sleep."

"God took on the entirety of the vow." I explained. "That means that it didn't matter if Abram was faithful to God, God would still make good on His promise. It meant that no matter what Abram or his descendants did, God would still keep His vow. If not, God would die. But God cannot die and God never breaks His promises."

Sarah smiled very big and bright. It seemed like a great place to end, didn't it? Talking about how God can never break His promises. Unfortunately for us, we had to end there whether we wanted to or not. Scoefield suddenly opened the door and slammed it behind him.

"Time for bed, pipsqueaks." He grunted.

And that was that. Bible study was over. And to my great regret, that was the last time we studied the Bible for a good while. Things, you could say, got busy.

CHAPTER TWELVE

Mr. Butters returned. His boss liked our song and the studio wished to make a deal with us.

We got Scoefield.

"What is this, Butters?" Scoefield eyed him as he walked out from the back of the diner. "I thought we already had our talk."

Fortunately, it was a slow day. Scoefield wasn't too busy.

"We did, Scoefield." Mr. Butters replied. "However, if I remember correctly, you said they could do one song and then we would talk."

Scoefield raised his eyebrows. From what I knew, that meant he was impressed.

"That we did, Butters." Scoefield nodded. "I appreciate ya' rememberin'. What'cha got for us?"

Mr. Butters motioned for us all to sit down at one of the tables. "I have great news for all of you."

He was whispering. I found it peculiar.

"Well?" Sarah asked, eagerly.

"Have any of you been listening to the radio?"

"Don't have one." Scoefield mentioned.

"Well, your song is all over it!" Mr. Butters exclaimed, still whispering. "People love it! In fact, people are wanting to have a…"

Mr. Butters paused, glancing at Scoefield. His foot began to tap.

"A live performance."

Scoefield's face remained unchanged. He stared at Mr. Butters with a cold, emotionless stare. Sarah and I looked at each other and then back at Mr. Butters.

"They want us to sing at the studio again?" I asked.

"No." Mr. Butters clarified. "They want you to sing at a concert. In front of people."

Silence. Scoefield said nothing. Sarah said nothing. I said nothing. I think it bothered Mr. Butters a little bit, so he continued talking.

"An-and we would *love* to be willing to give you enough incentive in order to allow this." Mr. Butters babbled. "Plus we could use more songs that you write up for us, Henry."

Still silence. For a few moments, in fact.

Mr. Butters was tapping his foot furiously.

"How much 'incentive'?" Scoefield finally broke the silence.

"Enough money to get you out of the Hooverville." Mr. Butters promised.

"I want it in writing." Scoefield jabbed a finger at him. "And *signed*."

"Done." Mr. Butters squeaked. "So…we can go forward with the concert idea."

"Ask them." Scoefield pointed his thumb at Sarah and I.

Mr. Butters looked at us.

I looked at Sarah.

Sarah looked at me.

I looked back at Mr. Butters.

"Why not?"

We received a good deal of money from that deal. It was quite incredible. We were making money. *I* was making money. Not just Scoefield. People loved our song! And I was able to continue writing songs for them. We were able to save up tons of money! Buy nice clothes! Eat good food! It was amazing! God was blessing us beyond what we ever thought. And the most incredible part was

168

when me, Sarah, and Scoefield all had a discussion one night about our financial situation. We were making good money, but we needed to think about how we would spend it.

"A house." Scoefield put forth. "A *real* house."

"You mean, out of the Hooverville?" I asked.

"Yeah." Scoefield nodded solemnly. "I'm tired of livin' in this pit. We can make it if we use the money right."

"You really think we could actually save up enough for a house out of here, Bradley?" Sarah questioned.

"We know how to live dirt poor." Scoefield brought up. "We've done it for years. All we need to do is keep doin' it for a while longer while this song keeps bringin' in the dough for us. We save up and we get outta' here. And it doesn't have to be a nice house. It can be run-down, for all I care. We can live with that for a while, and we can fix her up if we need to. I'm just-"

Scoefield took a breath and glanced at me. A small smile tugged at the corners of his mouth.

"Hopeful, ya' know?" He finished.

Sarah and I simultaneously smiled in response.

So, that was our goal. And the money was coming in great enough that it could happen. *Never* was on the radio while Scoefield was at the diner. We were living like we always had, but only for a short while longer. We were possibly moving up to a better life. We were getting excited!

...And I was getting a little too big for my britches. I was beginning to think that I was something. That I was all that. That I was worth more than I really was. And I started going behind Scoefield's back with Sarah...

169

"We shouldn't be doing this, Henry." Sarah whispered. "We're just making sure I get dry." I excused. That morning, I had taken a bath. Truth was, I needed one. But I had ulterior motives. During the cold months, Sarah and I had this routine of warming the other up after taking a bath so we wouldn't get sick. However, it was October. It was cooler out, but not necessarily cold just yet.

Sarah gave me an annoyed look to my response. "You know what I mean. You didn't wash this morning because you really wanted to get clean. It's not even cold out yet." I swallowed. She was right.

"I like being close to you like this." I admitted.

"And I like it, too." She replied. "But that doesn't make it right."

"You smell very nice." I changed the subject.

"No, I don't." She looked at me like I was crazy. "The last time I had a washing was last week. I do *not* smell nice."

"You do to me." I smiled.

Sarah let out a sigh. "Well, you are biased."

"I don't care." I gently rubbed her cheek with my hand. "I love you, Sarah."

I could feel her melt at my words. Her eyes grew wide and I could feel her heart accelerate.

It was the first time I had ever said it to her.

"Oh, Henry. I love you too." She whispered back, barely audible.

I probably melted at her words, to be honest. But at that moment, I felt an urge. I felt it and I didn't fight it. I acted on it without thinking.

I kissed Sarah. On the lips. Oh yes, I kissed her. She didn't stop me. In fact, she could see it coming. She knew I was going to kiss her and her eyes only gleamed, as if to invite me to do it.

Sarah and I shared our first kiss on that day.

Now let me say something. There may be people that read this who are cheering at this moment. There may be those that are congratulating me for what I did. But when I kissed her, let me tell you that the only ones who were cheering were of Satan's ranks. The angels were not cheering for Sarah and I. Jesus was not smiling in approval at our actions.

Rather, God was sighing heavily, shaking His head. The Holy Spirit was trying to call out to our hearts, saying "Stop now! You're only going down a path that will lead to heartache!"

But we were refusing to listen. We were following our wishes.

Remember that as this story continues. You will see.

Later on that night, I gazed up at the stars. There were those who told me that a big bang had made all of those stars. Made all of the universe. Seemed downright nonsense to me. I knew when I looked at the stars that I was staring at God's handiwork.

And that night, those stars seemed mighty judgmental to me. As if they were condemning me with their glimmer and beauty.

I sighed. I knew why I felt they were judging me. It really wasn't them. It was my own conscience. It was the Holy Spirit inside of me. And the sin nature inside of me was warring against the Holy Spirit.

The Holy Spirit was saying "You did wrong. Repent before you go too far."

The sin nature was saying "You are okay. Things like this are meant to be enjoyed."

And they were tangling up like two men in a wrestling match.

And the winner depended entirely on me.

I shook my head, trying to get my thoughts away from my feelings.

"I'm failing." I said to God above. "*Failing*. I want her like a bear wants honey…I'm failing her. I'm failing You. I'm caving to sin that I never before had issue with. I like to touch her. And Paul said 'It is good for a man not to touch a woman.' Can I just be honest and open? Sarah and I, we're doing many things that should not be done between two people that aren't married. And right now, it's wrong. But if we were married, it wouldn't be. I…want to be married to her…"

I swallowed hard, as if there was a large piece of food in my mouth. "And…we don't have any parents with us. Mine or hers. So I know that I can't get their help. But I want You to lead me. I know…I know that I am fiddling with things I really shouldn't. Getting close to her…Such like that. I need You to help me. I need You to lead me. I don't want to be this man that I see myself turning into. I want to grow to be like my father. Please help me to control myself. And if she…isn't the one for me…Please tell me soon so I don't get too attached. I don't mean to ask that proudly. It's humble, Lord. I just don't want to love someone I'm not supposed to."

I paused. "Actually, I guess it's too late to not love her if I am not supposed to, huh?"

One of the hardest things on this planet is relationships. Relationships of all kinds: parents to children, siblings to siblings, friends to friends…but the most complicated relationship, I believe, is between a man and a woman that have feelings for each other. It's bizarre, yet exciting. New, yet frightening. Wonderful, yet dangerous. Strong, yet fragile. It's hard to explain, I suppose.

I didn't know how to handle my love for Sarah. I wanted to be romantic with her, but I was beginning to cross a line. A line that I was beginning to care less and less about. That wasn't the only time we kissed. Here and there, we dabbled in the dangerous area of physical romance. We would kiss one day, abstain another. At one moment, we knew what was right. At another, we didn't care. We were indecisive. I knew it would come back to get me. So, I tried different things. I tried not to be alone with her. Whenever we could, I tried to be out in public. At church, at the library, at the diner, anywhere.

Simple walks were even a good idea.

"I'm afraid, Henry." Sarah told me on one of our walks. "I'm afraid of the concert coming up."

"It will be okay." I smiled at her. "You have *Never* memorized."

"But I've never sung in front of so many people before." Sarah gazed up at me with frightened eyes. "Not while on a stage."

"I'll be there with you."

"But what if I mess up?"

"I'll be there with you."

"But what if-"

"Shhh." I shushed her gently. "You are worrying too much, Sarah. It's not for two more weeks."

"But it's just *two* weeks!" Sarah exclaimed. "I'm gonna' die!"

"No, you can't die." I frowned at her. "Who will go on walks with me?"

173

"Bradley will." Sarah grinned.

"I don't know if I want that." I replied, putting my hands in my pockets. "I think we're drifting apart."

"He thinks more highly of you than you think." Sarah told me.

"But what if he knew what I've…" I stopped. I didn't want to bring that up.

"It will be okay." Sarah promised.

"Now you're starting to sound like me." I nudged at her with my elbow.

"If I was starting to sound like you, I would sound like '*Hallo, ich heiße* Henry'!"

As Sarah spoke in German, she gave her most razor-sharp, angry-sounding voice I had ever heard.

"Germans don't **always** sound like that!" I pointed out while laughing.

"Oh, really?" Sarah laughed back. "Then how would you say it?"

"*Hallo, ich heiße* Henry." I repeated in my proper-sounding, German accent just as a man walked past us. Right then, something happened that most people would call a coincidence.

"Henry Engel?" The man that passed us spoke. "Little Henry, is that you?"

I was startled as I turned to face him. First off, this complete stranger knew my name. Secondly, he looked shockingly similar to my father. He had the same brown hair, and a face of similar likeness to that of Franklin Engel. For a moment, I thought my father had been revived from the dead. I simply stood with a shocked face until the man explained himself with five words: "It's me! Your Uncle Arthur!"

Arthur Engel. My father's younger and only brother. A missionary to South Africa, of all places. He left for South Africa around the same time my father left for Germany. The Engel brothers. Both missionaries. Had my grandfather been a more spiritual man, he would have been extremely proud. Now, Uncle Arthur was not married. A single white man in the jungles of Africa. Everyone expected him to die from disease, "savage natives", or fierce animals. If he wasn't to die, people expected him to return from the "sheer horror and disgust" of such a place. However, my uncle not only loved Africa and its people, but he was thriving there as well. The Africans loved this white man that brought news of a God above all gods. He had already evangelized seven different tribes by the time I was born.

God was working through my uncle.

However, because of his vigor for the ministry, I had only met my uncle once. I was about five years old and I didn't really remember it. Thankfully, Uncle Arthur remembered my face.

"Uncle Arthur?!" I gasped.

"Yes!" He shouted and ran up to hug me.

Arthur Engel was the only person left in my family. By this time, both of my grandparents were dead, on both my mother and father's side. Both of my parents were dead. My mother was an only child, so there were no uncles or aunts on her side. The only one left was Uncle Arthur. We were the two last Engels.

Uncle Arthur and I escorted Sarah home before catching up. She assured me she would be fine because Scoefield would be there in just an hour or so. We rode in a car that Uncle Arthur had been lent by a friend. I didn't

175

know where we were driving. Uncle Arthur told me it would be a surprise as we headed down a rural road.

"I'm sorry I didn't make it for the funeral." He told me as we headed down the road. "I didn't exactly find out until recently, and it's not the easiest to travel to America from Africa on short notice these days."

"I understand, Uncle." I told him.

"By the time I arrived here, you had run away from the orphanage you were staying at." He glanced at me. "You want to tell me why?"

"I was being bullied because I was German..." I muttered.

"By the boys?"

"And the staff." I told him.

Uncle Arthur grunted angrily. "You know, the more time I spend in Africa, the more I'm really starting to dislike Americans."

"They're not all bad." I replied.

"Hmm." Uncle Arthur muttered. "Well, Henry, I want to ask you something."

"Yes, sir?"

"Would you like to come to Africa with me?" He asked. "See, I'm actually leaving tomorrow. It was an act of God that I found you today. I would have come to you sooner if I had known where you were. After all, Africa is doing quite well. We don't get economic depressions where I'm at. We depend more on farms than stocks."

I thought on it. Africa. After all, Uncle Arthur was the only family I had left.

"Uncle Arthur?" I began to speak.

"Yes?"

"I think...I think God wants me to stay in New York."

"Oh?" Arthur gave a hint of a smile. "And why is that?"

176

"Well, that girl that I was with? Sarah?"

Uncle Arthur nodded. "Yeah, the girl you fancy."

I stopped for a moment. *"How could he have known that after only being with us for ten minutes?"*

But I didn't want to discuss that.

"I think God wants me to stay with her and her brother. The brother doesn't know God and Sarah is newly saved. I believe God put me in their life to witness to them."

"Are you sure you want to stay here in New York?" Uncle Arthur questioned. "Things will be hard for you."

"I know. Things already have been. But the best place and safest place to be is in the center of God's will."

Uncle Arthur's smile grew huge. "You are just like your father."

He suddenly pulled the car into a dirt road driveway. He parked it and we stepped out of the car.

Before us was my grandfather's house. It was lightly covered with snow, but other than that, it was exactly the same as the last time I had seen it.

"As it turns out, your father had a will written out before he passed." Uncle Arthur explained to me as he began to walk up the steps to the house. "Since your Granddad passed, Franklin was the owner of this house. In Franklin's will, he left it to you."

I was stunned. "Me?"

I began to follow Uncle Arthur to the front door. "But I'm only sixteen years old."

"I know." Uncle Arthur ran his hand over the front door. "That's why I technically own this house. You won't truly inherit it until you are eighteen years old."

That made sense.

"However." Uncle Arthur reached into his pocket. "I leave for Africa tomorrow. I have no need for this house. If you were going to come with me, I was going to sell it. But I knew in my heart you weren't going to. Call it a hunch. So, since you're going to stay..."

He pulled a key out of his pocket. The key to the house. He held it out to me.

"I might as well give it to you."

My breath was stolen from me. I didn't know what to say. I simply took the key. I looked at it as I turned it over in my hands.

"Am I...even allowed to own a house?" I said after a good silence. "Will the government let me?"

"I don't think the government will have a problem with it." Uncle Arthur smiled. "I'm paying for everything. Let's just say I'm renting it out to you, but it's also rent-free."

I clutched the key in my hands as I looked up to my uncle.

"Thank you, Uncle Arthur."

He smiled and we hugged once more.

CHAPTER THIRTEEN

"Bradley, Henry has a surprise for us and he won't tell me what it is!" Sarah immediately shouted once Scoefield got home from the diner.

"Oh, please, kiddos!" Scoefield grunted. "It's 11:00 at night! You have to start squabblin' right as I get home?"

"Scoefield, you sound like a parent." I laughed.

"I feel like one!" He growled. "Now why aren't ya' tellin' Sarah the surprise?"

"I was waiting for you." I grinned. "We got to take a drive, though."

"Ha-ha." Scoefield gave a fake laugh. "You're a real riot, Henry. We don't got a car."

"I do." I showed them the car keys. "But I have to return it in the morning. We better go while we have it."

Sarah and Scoefield both looked rather surprised already.

We headed out to my uncle's borrowed car.

"Henry, where did you get a car?" Sarah looked awestruck.

"Did you steal it, churchy-boy?" Scoefield looked excited.

"I didn't steal it." I opened the driver's door. "….However, I'm not legally allowed to drive this, so we can't let anyone know."

Sarah was instantly worried. "Henry, you're only sixteen, I don't think we should-"

"I'm in!" Scoefield hopped in the passenger seat. "Make sure you drive it fast!"

I couldn't help but laugh. Sarah grew quite pale.

"Don't worry." I assured her. "I can drive a car. Everything will be okay."

179

Without a word, Sarah hesitantly slunk into the backseat. I sat in the driver's seat.

"Seriously, Henry." Scoefield whispered to me. "Fast. Real fast."

"I don't think that would be a good idea, Scoefield." I replied.

"Henry, if you're gonna' illegally drive a stolen car, you just gotta' drive fast." Scoefield said.

"This car is *not* stolen." I eyed him.

"Fast, bucko." Scoefield smiled. "That's all I'm sayin'."

"I will drive the speed limit." I stated firmly.

...I drove it fast. Ten miles over the speed limit. Can you blame me? I was going to have the car for one night. Scoefield was exclaiming that I had finally become a man. Sarah was cross with both of us. But thankfully, no police pulled us over.

We arrived at my grandfather's house.

"Have we been invited to a dinner with a rich person?" Sarah looked even more worried than she had when she was in the car. "Oh, Henry! I'm not dressed for that!"

"Oh, hush, Sarah." Scoefield rolled his eyes. "It's free food and Henry doesn't look all that presentable either."

I remained silent as we walked up the steps.

"Did your Uncle Arthur invite us?" Sarah asked me.

"You have an uncle here in New York, Henry?" Scoefield piped up.

"He just found out he was here this afternoon." Sarah explained to Scoefield.

"Ya' don't say." Scoefield said as I unlocked the house.

We walked in. I turned on the lights. Sheets were over all the furniture and it was rather dusty, but still the beautiful house I knew.

"What is this?" Scoefield was confused. "Where's the grub?"

"I never said we were invited to a fancy dinner." I smiled brightly.

Sarah was starting to put the pieces together as Scoefield turned to me.

"Then what is this?" He squinted.

"Our new house." I beamed.

Sarah put her hands up to her mouth as tears were building up in her eyes. Scoefield's expression became that of total amazement. He began looking around at the immensity of the house.

"…What?" Was all Scoefield could say.

"This is my grandfather's house." I began to explain. "He was a rich man. When he died, it became my father's. When my father died in the car accident, he had in his will that this house would become mine, but I wasn't of age, so my uncle got it. My uncle found me earlier today. He's heading to Africa and won't be back in a long while. So, he gave it to me."

Sarah laughed joyously, seeming unable to hold in her excitement. Scoefield walked up to me.

"*This* is where we will live?" He breathed quietly.

I gave a simple nod. Without any hesitation, Scoefield grabbed both me and Sarah and hugged us tightly. He began screaming with joy, jumping up and down. Sarah and I began doing the same.

There we were: three kids, in a wealthy house, screaming happily and jumping up and down. We did that for a good ten minutes. Everyone was so happy.

And I knew that God had done it all.

That night was the first night in three months that I had gotten to sleep in my own bed. As I had that first night in Scoefield and Sarah's shack, I went over all the blessings that I had been given. I had two wonderful friends. I had a job with Scoefield. I was taking Sarah to church. We had a nice home, now. The blessings were just piling up.

The night had come. I looked at myself in the mirror. I was wearing a three-piece suit. A black suitcoat and vest with a white shirt underneath. To top it off, I had a nice big red bow-tie around my neck. I had not ever worn something so expensive and debonair in my life. It was given to me by Mr. Butters.

A knock came at my door. "Henry, ya' ready?"

"Coming." I cleared my throat.

I exited my room to find Scoefield dressed in similar attire. His suit was nearly identical to mine, with the exception of his bow-tie being a simple black instead of red. It was rather shocking, at first. His greasy hair was combed back. His face was washed. His shoes were shined, pants were ironed, everything about him just shouted "proper". He even stood straighter. Scoefield now seemed less threatening, more charming, upstanding, and even could pass off as a gentleman. I began to wonder if that was what I looked like.

"Ugh, these monkey suits, am I right?" Scoefield chuckled as he tried to loosen his collar a bit. "Too tight."

"They do seem…inappropriate for men like us." I admitted.

"Feels nice, though." Scoefield muttered. "Feelin' rich, you know?"

"Absolutely." I nodded. "Too bad we have to give these back."

Scoefield shrugged. "What else would we use 'em for?"

"I'm ready." Sarah suddenly spoke out as she entered the hallway.

My heart stopped.

Sarah was gorgeously adorned in a flowing rose-red dress and a black dress sweater. With every step she took, the dress would glide along gracefully. I couldn't take my eyes off of her.

At least, I couldn't until Scoefield elbowed me.

"Focus." He growled.

"But I am." I snickered.

He elbowed me again.

"Bradley, stop." Sarah scolded. "So…how do I look?"

"Mama would'a been proud, Sissy." Scoefield smiled genuinely.

Sarah beamed at that. Then she gazed at me. She may not have been asking me how she looked, but I wanted to tell her what I thought.

The only problem was that words failed me at that moment. So, all I said was:

"You're beautiful."

It felt too simple to me, but Sarah blushed and smiled. I suppose she liked it enough.

Mr. Butters was waiting for us when we stepped outside.

"My, you kids look like real winners!" Mr. Butters greeted us as he opened the car door for Sarah.

"Does that mean we were losers before?" Scoefield whispered jokingly to me as we got in the back of the car. I chuckled at that.

For the whole ride, Scoefield and Mr. Butters were the ones that were talking. Mr. Butters would be talking about something concerning where Sarah and I were going to be singing and Scoefield would respond with how rich people have it so nice.

Sarah and I?

We were silent. We were pondering on how we were about to sing before hundreds of people. Rich people. Rich people that looked at kids like us with disdain. Rich people like the hotel manager Sarah and I had run into.

So much of it was terrifying. I wasn't even that good of a singer, though I had been assured by a few people that I was. Sarah was the real star. I glanced over at her. Her face was pale and her feet were constantly sliding back and forth on the car rug. Her breathing was fast. Her eyes were wide open.

She was just as scared as I was. Maybe more so. I wanted to hold her hand to comfort her. However, I was afraid of what Scoefield would do if I did. Instead, I leaned over to her.

"Are you okay?" I whispered to her.

She replied by simply shaking her head from side to side.

"Don't worry." I tried to smile. "We will be okay."

"I feel sick." Sarah whimpered. "Henry…I don't know if I can do this."

"We'll be okay." I told her.

"I don't even remember the song, Henry."

184

"We are singing *Never*."

"I'll forget the words!"

"It'll be okay." I assured her. "I promise you, Sarah. It will all work out. It will be okay."

I wonder how much I believed in those words at that moment. I wasn't panicking, but I certainly was scared out of my wits. And with that sobering fire in my throat and head, the time between us getting out of Mr. Butter's car and reaching the backstage all blended together. Before we knew it, we were hearing the words:

"Okay, kiddos, you're on." Mr. Butters told us.

"Henry! Henry!" Sarah whispered, panicking. "I can't do this! I really can't do this!"

"Sarah, stop worrying." I tried to calm her down. "Trust me, it will be-"

Sarah suddenly threw up all over the floor. Everyone jumped, exclaiming with shock and disgust. After Sarah was done, Scoefield stepped up to her.

"Okay, that's it." Scoefield gently put his hands on her and began directing her to the bathroom.

"Wait, son!" Mr. Butters called. "They're on ***right now***!"

"Well, I guess they're not, Butters!" Scoefield yelled back. "She's sick, blubber-head!"

Mr. Butters turned ghastly white. His boss behind him started grating his teeth in frustration.

"I'm fired?" Mr. Butters choked out.

"You must be a mind-reader." His boss growled. "Maybe you could do that for your next job."

"No." I said to Mr. Butters' boss. "I have an idea."

"It's over, kid." Mr. Butters' boss told me. "Go home."

"Wait, sir." I pressed as I took a piece of paper out of my pocket. "This is a new song I wrote a couple of weeks ago. Give it to the pianist"

"Son...."

"Please, sir." I begged. "Just...allow me to try something. These people did come here for something."

Mr. Butters' boss glanced at the song I had given him. He peered back at me. Then he sighed, but nodded.

I headed out on stage.

Alone.

My heart was racing. My head was pounding. I couldn't hear anything. I couldn't see anything except for the microphone. If I focused on the crowd, I would probably have fainted. So I focused just on the microphone. I took it in my hands.

Then I saw them.

The crowd.

Hundreds of people staring at me. Rich folks. Men and women in fancy clothing.

Staring at me.

"*Please help me.*" I called out silently to God.

"Good evening, ladies and gentleman." My shaky voice spoke into the microphone. "My name is Henry Engel. Well, I suppose you all already know that since my name was announced before I came out here."

Some small chuckles here and there.

"However, you probably expected a young woman to be coming out with me by the name of Sarah Scoefield. I'm very sad to say that she has become very sick in the past hour and is unable to perform with me."

Most of the crowd made a concerned "Ohhh".

"But as I have heard in this wonderful country: the show must go on." I smiled. I glanced over at Mr. Holt. He nodded at me, showing me he was ready with the new music.

"Unfortunately, the song *Never* is not the song you will be hearing tonight. I need Sarah for that. But I do have a new song for you. It is titled *Thankful List*. I hope you can enjoy it as much as you have enjoyed *Never.*"

Mr. Holt began playing the piano. A soft, sweet melody began ringing throughout the theater. Once the introduction was completed, I sang:

"I remember
A time in my life when I had so much
So much blessings
Then it came
Disaster swept in and I lost all I had
And I was tempted
To dwell on all of my sorrow
To drown myself in loss"

I suddenly felt a surge of confidence and began to sing louder and stronger.

"But now, no more
Because through this door
I have so much to be thankful for
And that list is growing
Growing day by day
Day by day"

I looked over the crowd. The size of their numbers didn't scare me any longer. I was not afraid. I went on to the second verse.

"You may be there
Finding yourself in a world of despair
You feel so empty
But don't fret
God, He will lift up all who come to Him
Cast yourself upon Him
I know the pain, how it burns you
How it can hurt too much"

"But now, no more
Because through this door
You can find much to be thankful for
And that list can grow
It can grow day by day
Day by day"

"Through hardship, I have Jesus
Through heartache, I have Jesus
Through heartbreak, I have Jesus
And He lifts me up"

"We can focus on the problems
We can think on what's wrong
Or we still can be thankful
And lift up our song"

I closed my eyes and let my voice sound like a trumpet. The fire inside my heart was pouring into the music. I can only give the glory to God that I was singing so well and so strongly.

"Cry no more
Because through this door
We have so much to be thankful for
And that list is growing
Growing day by day
Day by day"

"Cry no more
Because through this door
We have so much to be thankful for
And that list is growing
It's ever growing
Day by day"

I completed my song. The crowd was applauding before Mr. Holt was finished with the piano. The next few moments were a blur to me. I simply bowed and left the stage without another word. My head was spinning and I was hardly taking in what was happening. Before I knew it, I was before a baffled Mr. Butters and impressed Mr. Butters' boss.
"Not bad, kid." Mr. Butters' boss told me. "You *just* wrote that?"
"I did, sir." I breathed.
"Good job." He smiled at me. Then he glanced at Mr. Butters. "Take care of him. This boy just saved your job." Then he simply walked away. Mr. Butters stared at me.
"You deserve a treat, Mr. Engel." He stated.
"Mr. Engel?" I raised my eyebrows.

"Anyone who sticks their neck out on the line for a bumbling fool like me deserves a title." Mr. Butters smiled big and bright. "What do you want? Anything, within reason."

"Henry?" Sarah approached me. Scoefield was right behind her.

"Hey!" I beamed, walking towards them. "How are you feeling?"

It was rather strange. Both of them were looking at me like I had just come back from the dead.

I blinked as they stared at me. "…What?"

"We heard you, boyo." Scoefield said. "We came back after Sarah was done pukin'. You knocked 'em dead. You knocked *us* dead."

"I wasn't that good." I mumbled.

"Yes, you were." Sarah said almost sternly. "You were amazing."

"Listen to your friends, Mr. Engel." Mr. Butters slapped me on the shoulder.

I was rather astonished. Sarah was biased towards me, that much was true. She would say anything good about me, even if it was an out-right lie. Mr. Butters was rather friendly, so I couldn't exactly imagine him telling me the cold-hard truth about my voice. Scoefield, however, told it how it was. He was rather blunt in nature. Yet, he said I was great. However, no more of it was said. We simply went out for hot-fudge sundaes with Mr. Butters. We talked. We had fun.

That was a rather extraordinary night.

Before I could go to sleep that night, a knock came at my door.

"Hey, Henry?" It was Scoefield. "You awake?"

I got out of my bed and opened the door. "Yeah. Are you okay, Scoefield?"

Scoefield definitely had a different expression on. He seemed calm, yet troubled about something.

"Can I talk to ya'?" He asked.

"Sure. Come on in."

Scoefield walked in and simply stood next to my bed.

"What's wrong?"

"I..." Scoefield took a deep breath. "I was thinkin'...maybe I could learn more about God from ya'...again."

I was surprised. I didn't know what to say.

"See, Henry..." Scoefield sighed. "I've been on my own with Sarah for...yeesh, how long *has* it been? Five years? Eight years?"

He scratched his head as he thought about it. "Whatever, it doesn't matter. A long time. And all that time, it's been hard. I've had to fight like a maniac to keep her safe and healthy. And even doin' all that, we were barely scrapin' by. Then you come along. And poof. Everythin' starts goin' swell. I mean, we got forty-three dollars on the first night we met you. Ya' bring in some extra money with your songs. Ya'...make Sarah happy. And now, this?"

He gestured around at the house we were in.

"And we don't have to pay a dime for it?" He said, amazed. "Someone's lookin' out for ya', Henry. Maybe...God is really what you say He is. You're...a good man, Henry. A better man than anyone I've ever met."

He placed his hand on my shoulder.

"If you want, ya' can marry Sarah." He smiled. "Heck, I *want* ya' to marry Sarah. I know you'll take care of her. And not only that, but I wanna' come to church with ya' this Sunday."

I couldn't believe it. I mean, I really can't explain how overjoyed I was at that moment. Scoefield had finally come around. He was going to come to church with me and Sarah. And not only that! He had given me permission to not only court Sarah, but to marry her!
Everything was going right!
Everything was wonderful!
And then...
Everything fell apart.

CHAPTER FOURTEEN

Tomorrow came. It was Sunday. Unfortunately, Scoefield was called in to work.

"But what about what you said last night?" I asked him as he was heading out the door.

"Hey, I can't." Scoefield told me. "I can't just say I'm not comin' in. I'll get fired. Next Sunday, I promise."

"You better." I pointed at him.

"I promise, Henry." Scoefield said again as he began jogging down the road.

"Hey, Scoefield!" I called after him.

"Eh?" He called back.

"Sarah and I will drop by tonight to see you!"

"Yeah!" He shouted back. "I'll be waitin' for ya'!"

I went back inside the house. "Sarah! Are you coming?"

"Still waking up." She called from her room. "Why are we up so early? I need coffee."

"We've got a long ways to walk." I said as I climbed the stairs. "It will take us a lot longer to get to church."

I could hear her groan from inside her room.

"Come on." I told her from the other side of her door. "Hurry up, sleepy head."

The walk was definitely longer, but because we left early, we made it right on time. Now, I should be clear about why I have barely mentioned church in this entire story. Probably seems odd, doesn't it? A Christian boy who is so concerned with going to church, yet there's no account of church-going as of yet. To be honest with you, that's simply because there was nothing pertinent from my church experiences to the overall story. I heard wonderful sermons that touched my heart with correction, instruction, rebuke, and encouragement. But those are for me. You may or may not get the same results as I had with those sermons. However, this church experience is vital to my story.

Sarah and I sat down as Pastor Benson stepped up to his pulpit.

"Turn to Proverbs chapter 18, if you would." He began. "Proverbs 18. The Word of God through the Holy Spirit certainly gives us many things to ponder. Our text begins in verse 16. The title of our message is 'Build Bridges, Not Walls'. I hope to explain what I mean by that title. So, let's pick up our reading in verse 16 of Proverbs 18."

Pastor Benson straightened his glasses as he read out of his Bible.

"'A man's gift maketh room for him, and bringeth him before great men. *He that is* first in his own cause *seemeth* just; but his neighbour cometh and searcheth him. The lot causeth contentions to cease, and parteth between the mighty. A brother offended *is harder to be won* than a strong city: and *their* contentions *are* like the bars of a castle. A man's belly shall be satisfied with the fruit of his mouth; *and* with the increase of his lips shall he be filled. Death and life *are* in the power of the tongue: and they that love it shall eat the fruit thereof'."

Pastor Benson glanced up from his Bible, gazing out at all of us.

"I'm really going to focus on verse 19 for the majority of the message. It mentions contentions and it mentions a brother offended. All of us our going to deal with conflicts. I hope this will be some practical help here to each and

every one. Build bridges, not walls. May God bless the reading of His Word as you're seated."
We all sat down and awaited Pastor Benson to continue. Pastor Benson seemed rather heavy with some invisible burden that morning. He took an unusually long pause, just looking out at the congregation. He took a deep breath as he placed his hands on the pulpit. We all knew, from the passage he had read, this would be a more sobering message.

"The Word of God gives us many examples of what we would call strained relationships. *Strained* relationships. Instances where people who loved each other didn't talk and didn't talk for a long time. Jacob offended Esau. Esau, of course, went to the extreme and wanted to kill his brother. He was so irate at what Jacob the heel-grabber did. He tricked him out of his birthright and tricked him out of the blessing. Esau was upset and truly, they didn't speak for twenty years. For twenty years! They had zero conversation. And Jacob didn't think it would go well when they did get reunited, but it did. When it says 'a brother offended is harder to be won than a strong city' it doesn't say that it would be impossible. It just says it would be hard. And what about Joseph and his brothers? Obviously, they didn't speak for a number of years. Just a strained relationship. Even after they had spent many years in Goshen, and when Jacob died, they still thought Joseph was going to take it out on them, but Joseph never intended that. He said it this way: 'You meant it for evil but God meant it for good'. He had a different perspective. How about this relationship: Absalom and Amnon. Amnon took advantage of Absalom's sister in a very perverse way and Absalom never forgave him of it. He was quiet about it for

195

a while, but eventually he took revenge on Amnon. That also generated a strife between David and Absalom and they didn't speak for years. Even our beloved Paul and Barnabas. They had a strained relationship. Even Paul. Can I say it that way? I mean, he's just as much as flesh as what we are and said he struggled with the flesh. But we tend to think of him as just a great spiritual giant. But *even Paul* didn't agree with Barnabas about the matter of John Mark and it caused a division to come between the two of them. An unfortunate strain. They were offended, evidently, so much they had to part ways."

Pastor Benson walked a short ways from his pulpit. He was, again, just gazing out at the audience. His eyes seemed to have a sorrowing gaze. As if he knew of this pain. As if he himself was in what he called 'a strained relationship'.

He continued after a long silence. "Now, perhaps, there's an instance of a strained relationship in your life. Perhaps someone that you've offended and they've shut you out. They've shut you out. It's not a pleasant experience. It's not a pleasant topic that I'm preaching. I'm just trying to be faithful to preach through the Word. I think we need all of the counsel of the Word of God here."

A few men called out "Amen" at that.

"You may have someone that has shut you out. They don't return your letters. They no longer talk to you when they see you. It may even be somebody that's right here in the auditorium today that you haven't talked to in a long time. Is that right? It's not right. But is it possible? Highly possible. Hey, listen, we can be hurt. We can be hurt. Within a marriage, you can be hurt. Within a parent-child

relationship. Within a parent-*adult* child relationship. Friends, the best of friends, can hurt one another."
I began to tune out of the message. I had heard the word "marriage" and immediately began thinking about the wonderful woman next to me. Scoefield had given me permission to ask her to marry me. Besides, I didn't have any strained relationships in my life. This was certainly a message I didn't have to listen to.

"Maybe you've shut somebody out of your life." I started to tune back into the sermon. "You have nothing to do with them right now. James said it this way: 'In many things we offend all. If any man offend not in word, the same is a perfect man, and able also to bridle the whole body.' Then he goes on about the tongue and talks about it is a little member, but it does cause a whole heap of trouble. Since we are imperfect people, there will be offenses that occur as a result of either what is said or what is done, or what is *not* said or what is *not* done. Our natural tendency is to build defenses when we've been offended. Castles have been built. Some magnificent, amazing structures that have been built in England, and Scotland. Many, I saw, pictures of castles in India. Many all over the world. Fortifications have been built. Why? Why were they built? Many of those were built because people got offended."

I raised my eyebrows. I whispered to Sarah "There are castles in India?"
She shrugged. "How should I know? You're the one who's been on the same continent as India."
"India is in Asia. Germany is in Europe." I corrected.
"Shh." Sarah hushed me. "Listen to the sermon."

197

I obeyed and turned my attention back to Pastor.

"Gates have been barred. I really want to drive home this truth that in our relationships one with another, whether within a family, or within a friendship, or in a church family, or at the workplace that we all work to build bridges rather than walls."

Pastor Benson's voice echoed powerfully through the auditorium as we all took in his last statement.

"When someone says something or does something to hurt you, it's the most natural thing in the world for us to build a wall and say 'okay, that's it. I'm done with you.' That's obviously not the biblical response."

Pastor Benson then repeated the verse. "'A brother offended is harder to be won than a strong city: and their contentions are like the bars of a castle.' Solomon is communicating with his son and with us here today to help us in our interpersonal relationships so that we wouldn't offend one another, but also if having offended someone or having been offended, how to deal with it. Let's look at a few of these verses together. 'A man's gift maketh room for him, and bringeth him before great men.' Now, what is this saying? A gift given with a clear and sincere motive, a motive of love that says 'I care about you and I care about a relationship. I want to see things work out right'. Whether that's roses from a husband who said the wrong thing to a wife – hey, it doesn't hurt, right?"

My ears perked up at the word "wife". I glanced at Sarah next to me.

How I wanted her to be my wife.

"Or whether it's a gift given to a neighbor. A gift to say 'Hey, I'm sorry'. The wise men brought a gift before Christ

198

when they came. Jacob gave a very sizable gift to Esau. He gave him 550 animals when you add them all up. Jacob also sent a gift to the ruler of Egypt. He sent a gift. It was part of their culture. Part of the eastern mindset. If you come before a dignitary, you bring a gift. If you come before someone you love and respect, you bring a gift. It's saying 'Hey, we appreciate who you are. We're thankful for a relationship'. It opens things up. Here's one point I want to make: good communication will cost you. Good communication will cost you. You will pay a price for good communication. Point one being made: gifts can open doors of communication. Build bridges, not walls. If you've offended someone and they have set up a wall against you, then it is not wrong for you, (in love, not manipulation) to say 'hey, I'm sorry. Would you forgive me? I care about you and I care about a relationship' and send a gift. I'm just trying to be practical today, that if there is a strained relationship between parents and children, even adult children, that a gift could be in order there. It could open a door of communication. Does that make sense?"

Pastor waited for a moment. No one said "no", so he continued.
"All-right, let's go to point number two. Make sure you've heard both sides of the story. Build bridges, not walls. Listen, if you only hear one side of the story without hearing the other side, and you form an opinion before you hear the whole story, you've just built a wall. So, let's say your kid comes in and says 'my sister just hit me in the eye in with the toy!'. And you say 'Bless your little heart, they hit you? They will pay!', but then you find out he got hit because he took the toy in the first place. Now that doesn't

justify getting hit, but it makes a difference, doesn't it? Build bridges, not walls. Don't form an opinion before you hear both sides of it. Now could you be offended because of a misunderstanding? Could you be offended because you've really only heard one side of the story? Maybe you've heard your son's side of the story, but you haven't heard your daughter-in-law's story. Or maybe you've only heard your daughter's side of the story."

Pastor Benson chuckled some as he thought on that scenario. "Oh no. The daddy bear comes out. 'He said *what* to my little girl?'. But you better make sure you hear the other side of the story, because otherwise you just built a wall. If people are good-hearted people, and I realize that at our heart, we're not. The heart is wicked, isn't it? But we're talking about being believers. This is guidance and counsel for those who name the name of the Lord. So if it is Christians involved, then it ought to people are willing to hear people out and not make such hasty judgments. Wouldn't this help in the workplace? If before you come to a swift conclusion, you sit down with the individual and seek to understand where they're coming from and how the situation is from their perspective. It might help you to be a little more balanced. You got to hear both sides. You got to hear both sides. Number three. Number three comes from verse 18, it's this: look for a peaceful settlement. Look for a peaceful settlement. Build bridges, not walls. Paul said 'as much as lieth in you, live peaceably with all men'. Now, it didn't say you have to like all men, but he said live peaceably with all men. You may not like the person's personality. You may not like where they're coming from. You may not like a lot of things about them. But listen, we as believers need to make an effort to live peaceably with all men."

Pastor Benson pointed back at his Bible. "Look at verse 18: 'The lot causeth contentions to cease'. The lot. It was a small stone used to make impartial decisions and selections. For example, the land of Israel was divided by lot. There wasn't a big fighting about 'well, I want more of this land!'. They put the matter in God's hands. You know, that's what will help contentions to cease. When you put the matter in God's hands. Isn't that easier said than done? The sin of Achan was discovered by lots. The sailors determined who they were going to throw overboard by lots. You say 'Yeah, I like that idea'. No, don't take it too far, now. The idea is that they were going to allow for an impartial decision to be made. We don't really operate by lots today, unless you count flipping a coin. Or paper-rock-scissors. Or choosing a number between one and ten. It's using a kind of a lot. Somehow, there's got to be a peaceful settlement. I'm not saying choose numbers or draw straws. I'm saying this: search the Word of God to see if God has already ruled on that matter. Search the Word! See if God has already had something to say about that, and if He has, go with what God says. Don't try to shut the person out. Try to come to some type of an agreement where you'd say 'Let's look and see what God's Word says'. Now, you cannot determine what the other person is doing. You can only do your part to make sure that you are responding biblically according to what God wants."

Pastor paused again before continuing. "Cause the contention to cease. That's the goal. Ask yourself 'Am I building a wall or am I building a bridge?' There's obviously a contention here, there's strife here. Like Paul wanted for Euodias and Syntyche. That they be of the same mind. Somebody had to give. Somebody had to *for*give. Somebody had to ask for forgiveness. And probably both! What does unselfishness look like in that situation? We're so prone – *I'm* prone – to immediately build our defenses when we're hurt and not only our defenses, but we get out our bow and arrow! To hurt the one who has hurt us! Rather, we ought to put the matter in God's hands and, having done that, see what the unselfish thing would be to say or do and follow that. Trusting that God can mediate. Have you built a bridge or a wall? As a believer, we need to come to the place where we're willing to suffer loss. Whether it's financial loss or some other kind of loss in order to gain a relationship. You say 'But if I do that, it almost feels like they get their way!'. Hey, listen, the Word of God is not counseling us to compromise on sin or sweep sin under a rug, but what it is saying is that we really need to trust that God's at work in this situation and not feel like I have to be the one who's avenging. And thus, build a bridge, not a wall. You say 'But, wait a minute, what if *they* build a wall?'. Then, they built a wall. Well, that was profound, wasn't it? Here's what I'm saying: somebody might shut you out, and you can't control that. But don't you, as a believer, shut somebody else out. Does that make sense? You say 'But preacher, they've hurt me!'. I understand that. I can't say I understand the intensity of that pain, because I haven't been where you are, but I would imagine that's real hurt. But that doesn't license you to build a wall there and have nothing more to do with them. Build a bridge, not a wall. In other words, just make things work out. Don't give up on the relationship. It's easier said than done, isn't it?"

Pastor turned back to his Bible once more. "Okay, well, we come to verse 19. 'A brother offended *is harder to be won* than a strong city'. Brother. Could be a blood-brother. Family member. In fact, one man said this: 'the nearer the relationship, the wider the breach'. The break. The hurt. Maybe I can say it this way: the closer the person is to you, the more it hurts. Again, whether that's a son, a daughter, a son-in-law, a daughter-in-law, a spouse, a parent, a co-worker, a fellow church-member, or a pastor. And the word 'offended' is literally the word for 'transgress'. When someone has sinned against you. When someone has trespassed or transgressed. 'A brother offended *is harder to be won* than a strong city'. In other words, he or she shuts himself or herself off, they block you out, they don't let you in, they don't talk, they don't look your way, they pass by without shaking your hand. Hey. Come on. Not good. Like a fortified city, they may try to shoot at you if you try to approach. I also think about this: it's a city. There must be people on the inside. If you are the offender, you are on the outside. But no doubt, they have people that are on their side. And they want to keep the people on their side. And suddenly, it's not just one person who has offended another, but now, other people are involved in this as well. That's how church splits begin to take place. Because one person has an offense with another person, then they pull in other people, and 'can you believe what they said?' and next thing you know, people are choosing sides. Battlegrounds are being drawn. Hey, that's not how brothers and sisters in Christ are supposed to operate. But at the moment, the hurt person thinks that defense is better than reconciliation. That's what they think. If we're all honest today, some would say they've been in that situation before where they were hurt. And you think 'I'm *not* going to talk to them because it hurt when I did the last time. Defense is better than reconciliation'. Now, deep down, I believe that the person knows better than that, but that's how you feel. That's how you feel. So what do you do if you are in that situation? Well, we better be careful not to offend a brother or sister, because it *is* harder to win them back. So, the implication would be this: we need to do our due diligence not to offend them in the first place."

Pastor Benson moved closer to us, to make sure we heard. "Let me run that by you one more time: Not to offend them in the first place! I'm not talking about doctrine and such. Doctrine is important, but I'm talking about beyond doctrine. Listen, we have been called to love as God loves us. I don't want to say something offensive to you and you ought not say something offensive to another person. We all know that those relationships that are closest can be such that real hurt can take place more easily. You live together, you've known each other a long time. You can kind of just spout off and say what you want to say. But, hey, those words can hurt. They hurt deep. What if you were locked out of somebody's castle? I know I read in Song of Solomon how that their honeymoon is recorded in chapter 4 and even into chapter 5:1. But at 5:2, the honeymoon, friend, is *over*. And they're upset and he's outside and his hair is wet with the dew! The drops of the night. We say it this way: he's in the doghouse! He's locked out of her world. She's in bed and says, essentially, 'I'm not getting out of bed for you!'. Well, he then goes down to the garden, which I understand. There are times

when it's best to not talk right then. Everybody with me?
It'd be better to take some time to cool down. That can be
helpful. But that ought not take weeks. You must've been
really hot if you've been cooling down for weeks. Months.
Years. Something's wrong there. So, what if you have
offended someone? First of all, make sure you have taken
care of that offense right here."
He pointed towards his heart.

"Because any offense is ultimately between you and
God. That's the right place to take care of. Then, do what is
right regardless of the outcome. Forgive them. Love them.
Pray for them. Speak to them. 'What if they don't speak
back to me?' You still be friendly. I'm not saying write
them fifty times a day. That would be more offensive! Do
what is right, but you might say 'They won't reciprocate
that! They won't do right on their side!' Well, that then is
not your problem. That's their problem. Admit where
you've been wrong. Make your reconciliation a priority. In
fact, Jesus said 'Leave there thy gift before the altar, and go
thy way; first be reconciled to thy brother'. Don't move on
without that. Don't give up on the relationship. Don't give
up on the relationship. It *is* hard."

Pastor Benson glanced at the clock and realized the
time. I didn't mind. I really enjoyed the message.
"Okay, we need to do this quick." Pastor Benson flipped
through his Bible. "Luke 17. Can you do that? Turn to
Luke 17. Luke 17 and verse…well, really, the first five
verses are just amazing. Jesus is helping His disciples to
know how to deal with life when they've been offended or
when they've been offended. He says 'It is impossible but
that offences will come: but woe *unto him,* through whom

they come!'. This overlaps with Matthew 18. 'It were better for him that a millstone were hanged about his neck, and he cast into the sea, than that he should offend one of these little ones.' Hey, let me just pause right there to say God in heaven knows about the offense. He knows who's offended who. In fact, He knows better than what you and I do. He knows better! And thus, He knows that if there's been an offense, He's not overlooking that. You may feel like He is, but He's not really overlooking that. In fact, Jesus said it'd be better that he was thrown in the midst of the sea. You might say 'Yeah! I wish that would happen!' No, keep reading, keep reading. 'Take heed to yourselves' Jesus says. Take heed to *yourselves*! Your passions could overrule your reason! 'Take heed to yourselves: If thy brother trespass against thee,…' what does it say? 'Rebuke him'. Go tell him. Go tell her. Notice that it did not say 'If thy brother trespass against thee, take seven years to stew on it. Think about how bad it is that they said or did that. Go clam up about it'. No, the Bible doesn't say that. It actually says to go and talk to him about it. Go and talk to her. Again, it's parallel to Matthew 18:15 that says 'Go and tell him his fault between thee and him alone'. It does not say 'Go and broadcast it to everybody else', but rather, go to that individual. And say 'You know, I may have misunderstood things here'. That's a good place to start. Instead of coming in and say 'You know, you-!'. Okay. If you come in saying 'You!' then arrows are coming. They're already in defense. But if you say 'Because I care about a relationship, I want to try and clarify a few things that I may have totally misunderstood your motive or what you were saying. But I need to tell you that when this was said or done that it did hurt'. That's not being a baby about it. Everybody with me? That's being honest about it. 'It did hurt. It did put something between us. I want to get it solved. I want to get it right'. And so, the Bible says 'Rebuke him; and if he repent', look at the next words. If he says 'You're right, I'm wrong', look at the next verse. What does it say next? 'Forgive him'. And Jesus didn't stop there. Look at verse 4 'And if he trespass against thee seven times in a day, and seven times in a day turn again to thee, saying, I repent; thou shalt forgive him.' Whoa! No wonder the disciples said in the very next verse 'Lord, Increase our faith!'."

Pastor Benson took a moment to pause, then he took yet another long glance around the auditorium. "Don't give up on the relationship." His voice echoed. "I said don't give up on the relationship. Don't attack their castle. Don't think you're going to come in by storm and get them to get the drawbridge down. No, they're going to have to open the drawbridge to you. You do everything in your circle to make sure you are building bridges, not walls."
Another long pause. I looked around at others in the audience. Some people were leaning forward, as if to catch every word Pastor uttered. Others seemed disinterested. Probably how I looked. I admit that I wasn't as captivated as I should have been. Sarah…she seemed deeply interested in everything Pastor said.

"Hatred stirreth up strifes but love coverth all…sins." Pastor Benson gave a smile as he quoted Proverbs 10:12. "'Sins' is the same word as 'offended' in chapter 18. So, now, what if you're the one who has been offended. I think you've already gathered the thought from this, but I do want to try to briefly drive it home. I know we're right at

11:45. I usually try to get you out a little bit early. Is everybody all-right? How about we go to 1:00? Would you be offended if I did?"

The audience, along with the pastor, let out a laugh.

Pastor Benson immediately got serious again. "What if you're the one who has been offended? Well, based on these verses, I think what you ought to do is open the gate. Let the drawbridge down. Let them in. You say 'You got any more verses about that?'. Well, in Philemon 1:5, Paul says 'Hearing of thy love and faith, which thou hast toward the Lord Jesus, and toward all saints;'. Now what he's saying there is 'Philemon, I know your love, your faith in Jesus, rather, produces love for all saints'. And the book of Philemon is saying this: 'I want to tell you who's a saint now. Onesimus. The one who hurt you. The one who offended you'. And Paul is writing this to him to say 'You need to forgive him. Receive him as a brother'."

Pastor then walked down from his pulpit. Down from the podium. Down from the stage. Right down to our level. He began walking down into the aisle. He was on our level, as if he wanted to say 'I'm right here with you'.

"You may need to open your strong city. Unlock the bars of your castle. Be restored to your father, your mother, your father-in-law, your mother-in-law, your brother, your sister, your friend, your fellow church member. Because it sure is lonely in a solitary castle. It sure is lonely. 'Yeah, but I'm safe here'. It sure is lonely. Plus, you can't please the King. *The* King."

Pastor Benson pointed up, signifying that he was talking about God.

"You know, I thought about it this way: Aren't we blessed that God does not treat us like the offended brother in this passage? You know, He could have kept us out of His strong city. Instead, He sent His Son. He could have shut the door and barred the gate to that heavenly palace, but instead He sends out an invitation to all offenders. It's really going to come down for you and for me, the right choice of words. You see there in verse 20 'A man's belly shall be satisfied with the fruit of his mouth; and with the increase of his lips shall he be filled'. An agricultural example that is given. Fruit would be like from an orchard. Increase would be like from a field. Words have consequences. In a positive fashion. This problem can be rectified. It can be resolved. It can be restored...if the words are right. Right words give life to a relationship. 'I forgive you' – life!"

Pastor suddenly raised up his right hand as he said "life".

"'I hate you' – death!"

On "death", he raised up his left hand.

"'I don't want anything to do with you' – death!"

Left hand again.

"'I'd like to talk to you' – life!"

Right hand again.

Pastor turned back to his Bible. "'Death and life are in the power of the tongue'. Thus, we better be careful how we use it. Your words can kill or heal. A right relationship with those you love begins with a right relationship with the God above. Start right there. Receive the grace and He'll give you the words to go to the brother you've offended and say 'I'm honestly, sincerely sorry and I'd ask you to forgive me for the wrong'. If you do that, then you're doing your part. If they don't forgive you, if they keep the walls up, at least you've built a bridge and not a wall. You may have to keep building a bridge and keep building a bridge. It may take...a long time to be reconciled. But it is right. And it does please God. Are you building bridges or walls?"

CHAPTER FIFTEEN

"I've got something very good to tell you." I said to Sarah as we walked up to the house. We left church early after the service to get home for lunch at a decent time. "Oh?" Sarah responded.

"Scoefield came to my room last night." I smiled. "And he told me something."

"Well don't leave me guessing." Sarah smiled back. "What did he say?"

I could barely contain my happiness. "He not only wants to learn more about God, but he even wants to come to church."

For a moment, Sarah became serious. "Really? He said that?"

"He did."

Then the smile came. "He said that?"

"Yes, he said that." I laughed.

"I can't believe it!" Sarah suddenly hugged me. "My brother wants to know about God!"

I hugged her back. "But he did say something else, Sarah."

She pulled away. "What? What else did he say?"

I took a deep breath. I knelt down, getting on one knee. I took her hand in mine.

Sarah's face began to glow red as she realized what I was doing. A look of surprise and anticipation flooded her face. She placed her free hand over her mouth

"Sarah, a couple years back, your brother and I talked about the possibility of me and you being together. Not just as friends. As husband and wife. That is, if you want."

I could feel my face burning up too.

211

"I know I don't have a ring for you, yet. But I will do my best to raise up enough money to buy you one. Even so, will you marry me, Honey?"

She spoke. I am quite confident that she uttered words. But to my horror, I couldn't hear them. I think it was partly due to the fact that her hand was covering her mouth. The other part of it was that she was so quiet.

So, like a numbskull, I had to ask...

"What?"

She took her hand away from my mouth. "Of course I will."

Those were the words I had been hoping she'd say for years.

And now I heard them.

What would you do?

Me? I kissed her. Just rose up and kissed her. And she kissed me back. So I kissed her back after she kissed me back...

And we began to hold embrace each other very tightly...

With more kissing...

A fire in my heart was raging. A longing in my being was becoming uncontrollable. I suppose the same was happening with her.

And then...

Well, I'm sure you are starting to get the picture. Sarah and I did something that no unmarried couple should do. God created physical intimacy for a man and a woman that were married. Not before.

On that day...Sunday, of all days...Sarah and I both lost our virginity.

I sat down on the porch. I was beat red in the face. I could feel the heat from it. Not from embarrassment. From shame. I felt empty. I had done something so very wrong. Panic, shame, fear, regret all swirled inside me like a horrible hurricane. I was trembling uncontrollably.

And I couldn't think.

I couldn't think about how Sarah was up in my room crying.

I couldn't think about how Scoefield would react.

I couldn't think about what great wickedness I had done. About how I had sinned against God.

I could only think guilt.

I never knew I could think an abstract thing, but I was. Guilt. It was like a colossal weight thrown on my shoulders, reminding me constantly of what I had done. In my mind, I was running. Running on a plain of nothing. Stuck in place, trying to get away from something that was inevitably going to catch up to me.

I was running nowhere.

Cold was creeping onto my body. Like a virus. Like sin itself, wrapping its chains around me and saying with a subtle voice "You are mine now."

What had I done? Why had I done it? Such betrayal to Sarah's honor. But worse, such betrayal to God. His goodness, His mercy, His blessings, His presence with me...I had destroyed that wonderful fellowship between myself and the Lord that very day. Something so precious that I wanted most, given up for what I wanted in the moment.

On the porch, I wept. "Oh, God, forgive me. Please forgive me. I'm sorry."

That sin still haunts me to this day.

"We're not going to tell Scoefield." I told Sarah.

It had been over an hour. Sarah was sitting on her bed, fully dressed again. Her eyes were red from crying.

"But Henry..."

"Sarah, if Scoefield finds out what we did..." I didn't have to finish it.

Sarah took a deep breath. "You're right. He'd be furious." She looked back at me. "Henry, I'm scared."

I couldn't refrain myself. I walked over to the bed and held her in my arms. "I'm scared too, Sarah. And I'm so sorry. This is all my fault."

"It's not all your fault, Henry." Sarah spoke softly. "I wanted it too..."

"But I started-"

"No." Sarah looked right into my eyes. "I'm not going to let you take the blame for this. I am guilty too. You did not rape me, Henry. I committed it just as much as you did."

First off, she was right. Second off, I knew I couldn't argue with her. So I simply continued holding her.

"What do we tell Scoefield, then?" Sarah asked me.

"Church went late." I nodded. "That's what we tell him. He'll believe that. Pastor Wayne Benson is long-winded anyway."

"Okay." Sarah agreed. "...Henry?"

"Yes?"

"Do you love me?"

"Of course, Sarah." I assured her.

"Are you going to throw me away when another girl comes along."

"Listen to me." I told her as I lifted her head up. "I love you, Sarah Scoefield, and that will not change until eternity ends. No other woman will ever have my heart. I will

214

marry you, someday. I will provide for you, laugh with you, eat meals with you, go to carnivals with you, take photographs with you, worry with you, raise children with you, grow old with you, and die with you."

Even in the midst of sin and guilty consciences, Sarah gave a heart-melting smile.

I couldn't help but kiss her again.

Scoefield had to work late, so we never saw him when he came home. I woke up early the next morning for work. I was getting ready in the bathroom, nervous as ever. I couldn't act like something was wrong. I had to act like everything was normal. Once I was ready to head to work, I noticed Scoefield was still sleeping, with his door open. I knocked on his door.

"Scoefield, you going to work?" I called.

Scoefield stirred in his bed. He lifted up his head with his eyes mostly shut.

"I decided to take a day off." He yawned. "The boss was okay with it."

I gulped, still nervous. "Right. Right then, I'll just head to work."

I turned around and was about to walk down the stairs.

"Henry."

I stopped. My heart started racing.

"You and Sarah. Why didn't ya' come to the diner last night, like ya' said ya' would?"

I turned around with an unusually casual face. "Pastor Benson went a little long. By the time he was done, the diner was closed."

Scoefield stared at me for a couple of seconds. "Okay." Then he flopped back in his bed.

I breathed a huge sigh of relief. And I headed to work.

If only I knew.

I came home that day, sure that everything would be fine. Sure that Sarah and I weren't going to get caught. Then the door opened as I walked up onto the porch.

"Oh, hi, Henry." Scoefield greeted me as I came to the door. "How was work?"

I smiled. "Same as most days."

Suddenly, Scoefield's face twisted ever so slightly. I could see anger. My smile faded.

"Are you okay, Scoefield?"

"Oh, yeah! Yeah!" He exclaimed with a fake smile. "Why wouldn't I be, huh?"

I kept quiet. Something was wrong.

"Hey, uh, Henry." Scoefield's anger began to show more. "That preachy thing you took Sarah to last night? You said the preacher went long?"

I gulped. "Yeah."

"How long?" Scoefield interrogated.

"Probably until 10:00 at night, I suppose." I lied. "I didn't really check the time."

"Wow. Ten o' clock?" Scoefield's eyes twitched with rage, but he kept the fake smile on. "That's late."

"...Yeah."

"Hm, well that *is* strange." Scoefield clicked his tongue. "Ya' know, I went to the church at 9:00 last night."

My voice quivered. "You did?"

"Oh, yeah. Yeah, I did, Henry." His eyes were blazing. "I didn't have to work late. They let me go early. I hadn't seen ya' or Sarah, so I thought to myself that you two were still at the church. I went up to the church, and it's the weirdest thing: the lights were all off, nobody was inside, the doors were locked."

I was sweating by this time. He knew.

Yet, he continued. "But ya' know, I just thought that maybe Sarah wasn't feeling well, or you forgot or something. So I asked ya' this morning. When you *lied* to me, I asked Sarah. She said the same thing."

His fake smile was gone now. He was glaring at me with an angry scowl. His hands were in fists.

"So, I asked her why she was lyin'." His voice was low. I was preparing for the worst. "And ya' know what she told me?"

"Behold, ye have sinned against the LORD: and be sure your sin will find you out." I quoted Numbers 32:23 in my head.

I deserved punishment.

And it came. Scoefield socked me in the mouth. I tumbled down the steps.

"She told me everythin', Engel!" He finally shouted.

I was bleeding. Scoefield had knocked a tooth out. But he wasn't finished. He pulled me back up to my feet and shoved me.

"There was *one* thing in this world, Engel! *One* thing I cared about! You went and touched my sister! You were my *friend*, Engel!"

"Scoefield, I'm sorry!" I tried to apologize.

"Zip it!" He put his fist next to my face. "I can't trust a word you say! You *lied* to me! You said you were a Christian! A God-honorin' man! What kind of man does *this*?! You defiled my sister! My *sister*! You don't care about nobody but yourself! You're just like my pop!"

"Scoefield, I-"

"Get outta' here, Engel." Scoefield pointed towards the road. "Go away. I don't ever want to see your face again. Get outta' here before I give you a reason to run!"

I paused. "What?"

He was telling me to leave.

Leave Sarah.

Leave my only home.

"This wasn't supposed to happen." I thought. *"This **can't** happen."*

"Get outta' here!"

There was no reasoning with him.

I began to cry. "Scoefield..."

"If you cry, I swear, I'll break your nose." Scoefield threatened. "Last time I'm sayin' it, Engel. Leave."

"Not without me." Sarah's voice came from the doorway. Scoefield and I turned to see Sarah wrapped up in a coat with a bag in each of her hands.

"Sarah, what're you doin'?" Scoefield breathed, frustrated. "Get back in the house."

"No." Sarah stood firm. There were tears in her eyes as well. "I'm going with him."

Scoefield was awestruck. He climbed the steps. "Hey, hey, Sarah...You can't go with this guy. He's...he's a liar. He...ya' know what he did to you."

"I chose to do it too, Bradley." Sarah told him.

"No, you're stayin'." Scoefield ordered. "He's gonna' leave you at the first sight of trouble. He'll dump you for floozy dames. You can't trust him."

"I love him." Sarah whispered. "And he loves me. I'm going."

Scoefield was silenced. Sarah began walking past him, down the steps.

218

Towards me.

"Sarah, Sarah, you're gonna' choose him? Over your own brother?" Scoefield asked her.

Sarah ignored him, continuing towards me.

"Sarah, we're family!"

"Yes!" Sarah spun around, screaming. "I choose him! I chose him a long time ago! I lied to you, too, Bradley! We're both liars and we're both fornicators! I'm *going* with him!"

Sarah turned back around to me. She had tears pouring down her face.

"I choose you, Henry."

It's hard to explain what I felt right then. Sarah Scoefield was choosing to let go of the only family she had left. She was willing to say goodbye to Bradley Scoefield, her brother, in order to be with the sinful saint.

Henry Engel.

Conflict was raging on inside me. Sarah should never have had to choose between family and love. God never designed for it to be that way. Sarah should have had both. Her brother and me. And, because of my actions, because of my selfishness, because of my impatience…

She was forced to choose.

And she chose me.

Don't get me wrong, I was happy she chose me. I wanted her to choose me. I loved her. I wanted to marry her.

But I saw Scoefield's face. A face warped and distorted by so many emotions. Scoefield looked as if he had just been betrayed. As if his sister had been stolen, snatched away, from him. The one thing he protected so carefully

throughout his entire life was taken from him by his best friend. Scoefield shook his head slightly, as if he wasn't believing what was happening. I knew that feeling. It was the same feeling I had when my parents were killed.
And now, Scoefield was watching in disbelief as he was losing his sister. Like she was dying, and the killer was me. Then his eyes met mine. He let out a hot breath. I could see the storm billow in his eyes.
Then he charged for me.

Shoving Sarah out of the way, Scoefield tackled me to the ground. I hit my head hard on the gravel, and before I could recover, blows were landing on my face.
"I trusted you! I opened my life to you! You were my friend! How could ya' do this to me?!"
He kept shouting. Ranting and raving at me. My nose was bleeding, I could tell. My eyes were swelling from his punches. They would most likely be shiners before the night was over.
"Bradley! Get off of him! Get off of him! Please, stop, Bradley!" I could hear Sarah plead.
I opened my bruised eyes. Scoefield hesitated for just a moment, looking at Sarah, who was pulling at his shirt.
I palmed my fist and struck Scoefield right in the nose. I felt something crack and he fell off of me.
Sarah immediately came to help me. "Are you all-right, Henry?"
I wiped the blood coming from my nose. "Yeah."
I sat up, noticing Scoefield was wiping blood from his nose as well.
"You broke my nose, you stinkin' grifter." Scoefield grumbled.

"You were asking for it!" Sarah shouted in my defense. She helped me stand up. "Leave us alone, Bradley! Stay out of our lives!"

"You're not goin' nowhere!" Scoefield shouted, standing to his feet.

"You can't stop us, Bradley!"

"You're keepin' the house!" Scoefield shouted back.

Sarah and I were both stunned.

"I'm the one who's leavin'." Scoefield glared at me.

And without another word, Scoefield stormed off. Sarah eventually called after him.

But he did not stop. And he didn't respond.

CHAPTER SIXTEEN

"This should help." Sarah told me as she placed a raw steak on my right eye. We only had one steak in the ice box. Sarah told me I should put in on my right eye, seeing my left one wasn't as bad.

"You think he's going to be okay?" I asked Sarah as I held the meat against my eye.

"Bradley always gets furious when it comes to me." Sarah sighed. "Of course, nothing like this has ever happened before. I'm...not sure what he'll do."

"Do you think he'll come back?"

Sarah shook her head. "I don't know. We just need to give him time to cool off."

"And pray for him." I added.

Sarah gave me a guilty look. "Will God even listen to us, Henry?"

That question took me by surprise. "What are you talking about?"

"You know what we did..." Sarah looked away. "Will God even forgive us?"

I reached out and took a hold of her hands.

"1 John 1:9 says 'If we confess our sins, He is faithful and just to forgive us *our* sins, and to cleanse us from all unrighteousness'. He will forgive us, Honey. We just need to go to Him in prayer and confess what we've done."

I set the steak down. Sarah and I knelt down right there and began to pray.

"You go first." She whispered to me.

I took a breath as I closed my eyes. At certain times when I was to pray aloud, I always tried to plan out what I was going to say. I made sure that I prayed like a godly man would pray. I said spiritual things like "bless our nation" or "keep a hedge of protection around us" or something of that nature. But right at that moment, I knew I couldn't pray in that hollow jargon.

I had to pray from my heart.

"Lord." I began. "I messed up. We messed up. At the time...I didn't care. We just wanted what we wanted. And we got it. Now, I'm feeling so heavy. Heavy like a man that's wearing rocks for clothes. I want to take it all back. Scoefield is furious with me. And I should have known we wouldn't have been able to hide it from him. My sin will always find me out. I...have no true way to express what I'm feeling, but I mean this with everything in me: I am sorry. Those are some of the most over-used words in existence. But I mean them so much. I wish there was more I could say to show You how much I mean that. I want forgiveness. I want redemption. I know that, regardless of what Sarah says, that this was mainly my doing and my fault."

I heard Sarah give a ragged breath when I said that.

I continued. "But we both were wrong. And now, damage has been done that cannot be undone. But, Lord, I just ask You this: can you please forgive us and renew us? Clean our filthy hearts and allow us to go on in Your will, please, Lord."

A simple prayer. But a genuine one. To my great regret, I don't really remember what Sarah prayed that night. I know that it was beautiful and it was priceless like she is, but I can't recall the words. We never told Pastor Benson about what we did. We were so ashamed of it. Sarah never got pregnant from it. We thought it would be best to keep it between us and God.

For several days, Scoefield was nowhere to be found. He didn't come back to the house. He wasn't at the diner. He wasn't anywhere he normally would have been. Sarah and I were becoming quite worried. One week, two weeks, three weeks passed by.

No sign of him.

On the brighter side, Sarah and I became closer than ever. We had to. She had no brother to turn to anymore. I had no best friend. And we both felt that it was better to get married sooner rather than later. After all, we were both living alone in the same house and in love with one another.

On May 17th, 1934, Sarah Scoefield walked down the aisle of our church.

Sarah Engel walked out the doors of that church.

And that was the hardest year. We were newly married and the Depression was only getting worse.

And we didn't have Scoefield.

To this day, I felt like God was punishing me in that year, making me work three times as hard as I had ever worked. Thankfully, Sarah and I still didn't have to pay for the house. Uncle Arthur was taking care of that. But food? Heat? Oh, it was rough. It was stressful. Every night, as Sarah slept, I would pray. Pray words to God that would end the pain I had. The pain of losing Scoefield. The pain of working...so very hard. The pain of worry. The pain of exhaustion. The pain of regret. One night, I worked my prayers into two songs. One was for God.

FORGIVE ME ONCE AGAIN

I'VE STRAYED FROM THE PATH THAT YOU FIRST PUT
ME ON
MY PRIDE GREW TOO GREAT, NOW MY CONSCIENCE
IS GONE
EMPTY AND OPEN I COME
I CONFESS WHAT I'VE DONE
SAVE ME FROM THIS SINFUL DEN
LORD, PLEASE FORGIVE ME ONCE AGAIN

I'VE CARRIED MY CROSS FAR LESS TIMES THAN I
SHOULD
I'VE NOT BEEN THE MAN THAT I PROMISED I WOULD
I'M SHATTERED AND BROKEN WITHIN
AND I'M DROWNING IN SIN
I WANT TO COME BACK FROM WHERE I'VE BEEN
LORD, PLEASE FORGIVE ME ONCE AGAIN

I WAS WRONG
I WAS RUNNING
I THOUGHT I WAS OKAY
BUT IT WAS YOU I WAS SHUNNING
NOW MY HEART IS BLEEDING
I REPENT FROM MY SIN
YOU ARE WHO I AM NEEDING

I WANT TO BE BACK INTO YOUR LOVING ARMS

SAVE ME FROM THE SORROW, THE SHAME, AND
THE HARM
ALMIGHTY GOD, SAVIOUR, AND GUIDE
OH, HEAR MY HUMBLE CRY
YOU ARE MY MASTER AND MY FRIEND
LORD, PLEASE FORGIVE ME ONCE AGAIN

I WAS WRONG
I WAS RUNNING
I THOUGHT I WAS OKAY
BUT IT WAS YOU I WAS SHUNNING
NOW MY HEART IS BLEEDING
I REPENT FROM MY SIN
YOU ARE WHO I AM NEEDING

I'M FIGHTING, I'M STRUGGLING TO GET BACK TO MY
HOME
I KNOW IN MY HEART I CAN'T DO IT ALONE
I NEED TO FIND REDEMPTION
I NEED FORGIVENESS
I NEED A CURE FOR THIS SOUL-EATING SICKNESS

I'VE NOWHERE TO RUN, I HAVE NOWHERE TO GO
THERE IS NO ONE ELSE THAT CARES FOR ME SO
YOU ARE THE LORD OF ALL THINGS
THE MIGHTY KING OF KINGS
AND BEFORE YOU I HAVE SINNED

The other was for Scoefield. But we'll get to that later.

CHAPTER SEVENTEEN

One evening, about an hour after I had gotten home from work, a knock came at the door. I opened the door to find him. Scoefield.

I was so happy at first.

"Scoefield!" I beamed. "You came back!"

"Not for long, Engel." He sneered back at me. "Now, if ya' would be so kind, I'd like to talk to my sister."

My smile faded. "But Scoefield, I-"

"Oh, sorry." Scoefield said mockingly. "I gotta' ask permission, don't I? After all, she's *yours* now, ain't she?"

"No, Scoefield, it's not like that-"

"Get me Sarah, Engel." Scoefield ordered roughly. "And get outta' my face. And then, I promise you, you will never see me again. Got it?"

I wanted to say more. To try and plead with him. To try and revive the Scoefield I knew before my sin was discovered.

But I knew that I wouldn't be able to do it.

I left the front door and got Sarah. She ran to the door to talk to her brother.

I hid behind the stairwell to hear what they were saying.

"I'm leavin'." Scoefield said bluntly.

"You already did." Sarah sounded confused. "Why come back just to say that?"

"I mean I'm leaving New York." Scoefield clarified. "I'm joinin' the army."

"The army?" Sarah sounded worried. "Bradley, please! Don't do that! Please forgive us! Come back and live with us!"

228

"Don't ya' tell me what to do." Scoefield growled low. "Ya' chose him, ya' got him. Ya' don't need me. So I'm gone."

"You're going to get yourself killed, Bradley." Sarah said sadly.

"Well maybe I deserve that." Scoefield muttered.

"Bradley." I could hear Sarah begin to cry. "Please don't do this."

"Don't you cry in front of me!" Scoefield shouted. "It ain't gonna' work! I'm headin' out tomorrow and I'm not comin' back. So this is goodbye, Sarah."

"I don't want to say goodbye!"

"Well, too bad." Scoefield snarled. "And tell that grifter if he ever hurts ya' or if he ever leaves ya' for a floozy, I'll kill him. And I don't mean I'll beat him up. I mean I will end his life. Ya' got me?"

"Bradley…" Sarah sobbed.

"Goodbye, Sarah."

Then I heard him stomp off the porch. Sarah ran outside, crying his name. I slumped down to my knees, feeling filled to the brim with all manner of awful emotions.

I had done this. I had shattered my friendship with Bradley Scoefield. I had desecrated Sarah's relationship with her only family member.

"I'm sorry." I whispered to the air, as tears ran down my face. "I'm sorry."

Scoefield, if you are reading this, please come back. I beg you, please forgive me. I know you're angry with me. I know that you're holding bitterness against me. It will only hurt you more in the long run. I know I did exactly what you told me not to. But I want to make things right. I want to be friends again. If there is any possible way of that happening, I'll do it. I don't want to lose you. Please,

Scoefield. Let's build a bridge. Not walls. I have written this entire book just to say that I'm sorry and I want to be redeemed in your eyes.

Please.

Let the still waters that is our friendship run again.

The other song I talked about? I wrote it for you. I know you don't like poetry. I know you think it's a girly thing. But I wrote it for you.

<u>CONSEQUENCE</u>

GOD GAVE ME A BROTHER

THAT I DID NOT ASK FOR

A STRONG MAN, YET KIND

AND LOYAL AT HIS CORE

BUT ONE DAY I BROKE MY DEAR BROTHER'S HEART

WHEN I TOOK HIS FAMILY

AND TORE IT APART

I WAS FOREVER BANISHED FROM HIM ON THAT DAY

AND, WITH TEARS IN MY EYES, BROTHER, I WANT

TO SAY

CAN I BE REDEEMED?

CAN YOU COME HOME FROM WAR?

THIS ANGER, THIS HATE

DON'T HOLD IT ANYMORE

I JUST WANT TO MAKE IT RIGHT

I WANT TO SEE YOUR SMILE

FOR YOUR FORGIVENESS
I'LL WALK A THOUSAND MILES
I WAS WRONG
I WASN'T USING MY SENSE
BUT NOW I KNOW
THAT THIS IS MY CONSEQUENCE

GUILT IS HELD OVER ME
IT'S HEAVIER THAN LEAD
SORROW AND REGRET
ARE ALL THAT'S IN MY HEAD

DOWN ON MY KNEES, PLEADING OUT TO MY LORD
HE HAS FORGIVEN ME, BUT YOU
HAVE NOT SHEATHED YOUR SWORD

I CONFESS THAT I WAS IN SIN, I ADMIT MY EVIL
WAY
NOW, BROTHER, OH BROTHER, JUST HEAR ME
TODAY

CAN I BE REDEEMED?
CAN YOU COME HOME FROM WAR?
THIS ANGER, THIS HATE
DON'T HOLD IT ANYMORE
I JUST WANT TO MAKE IT RIGHT
I WANT TO SEE YOUR SMILE

FOR YOUR FORGIVENESS
I'LL WALK A THOUSAND MILES
I WAS WRONG
I WASN'T USING MY SENSE
BUT NOW I KNOW
THAT THIS IS MY CONSEQUENCE

I AM AS MOSES, OR DAVID, OR PAUL
MEN WHO WERE SINNERS
MEN WHO DID FALL
AND IT'S NO EXCUSE
FOR YOU NOT TO ACCUSE
BUT BROTHER, SINNERS ARE WE NOT ALL?

CAN I BE REDEEMED?
CAN YOU COME HOME FROM WAR?
THIS ANGER, THIS HATE
DON'T HOLD IT ANYMORE
I JUST WANT TO MAKE IT RIGHT
I WANT TO SEE YOUR SMILE
FOR YOUR FORGIVENESS
I'LL WALK A THOUSAND MILES
I WAS WRONG
I WASN'T USING MY SENSE
BUT NOW I KNOW
THAT THIS IS MY CONSEQUENCE

TO BE CONTINUED…

Please leave an honest review on Amazon
or send it to krohnstories@gmail.com
Every review helps and is appreciated!

BONUS MATERIAL

DON'T READ BEFORE READING THE BOOK. MAJOR PLOT POINTS FROM THIS BOOK ARE DISCUSSED. YOU HAVE BEEN WARNED.

Question & Answer

1. When did you first start writing/want to be an author?

It all began with an old computer my mom gave me when I was a young kid. It wasn't of any use to her since it was a bit outdated and it couldn't even connect to the internet. It was much more massive than many computers you'll find today. The monitor alone was about the size of a tire and it was heavy enough to be used as a cannonball.

Anyway, my mom let me use it regularly since I liked to use Paint to make pictures and whatnot. But one day, I started making little stories on Microsoft Word. Most of them were ridiculous and closely similar to Star Wars. But as time went on, I found that this was something I really enjoyed and I started become serious about my writing when I was in 5th Grade, which was 2005 for me. I began working relentlessly on a story that was titled Fantasy Fable. Sadly, it had to be thrown away in 2008.

But after quitting Fantasy Fable, Heroes & Thieves was the next story that I began writing. The idea for Scoefield came shortly after that. And today, there are now two books in the Scoefield series and almost three full Heroes & Thieves books out there! Took a while, but I can actually hold them in my hands now! It's a really good feeling.

If you aspire to be a writer, I would say go for it. I may not be a big shot, but I certainly can rejoice in the simple pleasures of completing my works and sharing them with others.

2. Did the events of Scoefield actually happen to someone back in the Great Depression?

If we're talking about the generic, historical things that took place in those times (job loss, destitution, hoovervilles, prejudice against African Americans and Germans[1], etc.), then yes. But if you mean more along the

1. These people groups are specifically named because they are the ones that are shown in Scoefield. This isn't to say that there was not prejudice against other ethnicities/nationalities in this time period.

lines of the events that specifically took place with Henry, Sarah, and Scoefield? No, not to my knowledge. That is just a fictional story I invented.

I was once asked by a dear friend of mine if Scoefield was based on a true story. She asked me this because she was in her upper 80's (this was several years back) and had lived during the Great Depression. Also, she was German, and had experienced much of the prejudice that Henry had. I was excited that she thought it was real because that meant it was convincing and that I was being credited as historically accurate by someone who *actually* lived in those times. All the same, no. It's not based off of a true story.

3. Where did you get the idea for Scoefield (the book)?

It actually came after I had been writing Heroes & Thieves for some years. The Heroes & Thieves books take much longer to finish because they're connected with The Zalian Chronicles, which is an entire literary universe. Much more to consider and a lot more work with the overall plot. Also, they're just plain bigger books. The

Scoefield Series was a much simpler story and it was originally going to be just two books. Not only that, but I wanted my first book to be dedicated to the Lord and Scoefield revolved around the Gospel whereas The Noble Bandit was more Lord-of-the-Rings-ish. But the idea for the Scoefield series originated out of some inner conflict concerning writing.

My first major story idea, Fantasy Fable, was acting as a distraction and it was keeping me away from the spiritual aspects of life, causing my walk with God to suffer as I fled away to a dreamland every day. There's nothing wrong with getting away from reality every now and again, but I was taking it to an unhealthy level. After I put the story away, I found that I wanted God to be a part of my writing rather than having the two divided. But, at the time, all that I was concocting dealt with very non-spiritual type stories.

But after going through a phase of watching World War II movies, an idea sprouted of a Christian man in the midst of World War II. So, honestly, the story of Engel actually came before Scoefield did. But I couldn't just start with a young man going into World War II without knowing anything about him. I needed some background information when he was a kid. Thus, I started jotting down notes of who this young man was and how he grew up in the Great Depression. Originally, Henry was going to be the only main character, but Bradley Scoefield came into the picture very soon since I figured that Henry would be trying to win someone to Christ. From there, the story just evolved into what it is today.

4. Are any characters based off of real people?

Not exactly. I would take snippets of personality from people I knew and throw some of that into a character. A really good example of this is Sarah. There's a lot of my wife, Marissa, in Sarah. Both Sarah and Marissa love snakes and sunflowers. Both can be rather shy, but can be scary and fiery when provoked. But they're still two different people. For example, Sarah is usually cold to people until she gets to know them while Marissa is kind to everybody.

Now, the two characters who are most closely based off of a real person would be Henry and Scoefield. They're based off of different aspects of me. And some people may think "Duh! You're the writer. *Everyone* is going to be based off of you in some degree". But Henry and Scoefield were more purposely fashioned this way. For Henry, I put more of my soft side into him. My kindness, thoughtfulness, creativity, smarts, fear, frailty, lovey-dovey-ness, etc. Every part of Henry is related to me in some fashion (except being German and speaking German. Sorry, that's made up), but everything that was left out of Henry was placed in Scoefield: my protectiveness, boldness, anger, sarcasm, diligence, wise-crackingness, etc. Put these two together and you get me, essentially. However, people have told me that I'm definitely more Henry than I am Scoefield, which I can't really deny.

5. Where did you get the name "Scoefield" and why does it have the extra "e"? Is there any special meaning behind it?

Funny story, I had no idea that Scofield/Schofield/etc. was such a prominent last name. I remember, back when I was in either middle school or high school, coming up with the name because of a great man in my church. He had been a colonel in the military and was a very authoritative, strong, and intimidating man (he was also very compassionate, but you wouldn't get that feel from first glance). I wanted Bradley to have a similar feel about him, especially for the sequel, so I borrowed part of his name. His last name is Mayfield and I liked the sound of it, so I put "Scoefield". And I thought that I completely made up that last name. That it had never been used before. Once I really started writing the book, however, I found about the Scofield Bibles and the multitude of people that had that as their last name. At that point, I had already gotten so used to the name that I couldn't think of replacing it. The "e" was just added because I thought it fit and it felt right to me.

The name Scofield means "dweller by a field with a hut", so it wasn't too pertinent to the book story. However, Bradley Scoefield was actually one of the *only* names that I didn't purposely put some meaning behind it. Almost every other name has some special meaning behind it:

Henry Engel: Engel means "Angel" in German. This is to reference how Henry was going to be the messenger of the Gospel through the story (Angel means "messenger" for those who don't know). It was also to connote that he would be the godly guy.

Sarah Scoefield: Sarah means "princess" in Hebrew. Since Sarah was going to be Henry's love interest, I wanted to provide a name that showed how he saw her. Also, I like the name. It's a good one.

Nancy Barber: Nancy means "grace" in Hebrew. I wanted Nancy, Scoefield's co-worker, to be shown as a truly gracious and kind woman. Even when dealing with the Tanner boys, she is polite. It takes a woman of strong character to be respectful to jerks like them.

Amos Scoefield: Amos means "burden" in some translations. I have found that there are some meanings where this is shown to be a positive thing, such as "carried by God", but I used this name so as to show how Amos was a burden to his family. Because of him, both Scoefield and Sarah had very broken childhoods that haunted them even into their adult years.

And (***hint, hint***) this might be a thing that continues in the Scoefield series. Take a look at some of the names and see if you learn something new about their characters.

6. What is Scoefield's accent? Why doesn't Sarah have it?

Technically, it's a Brooklyn accent, but it's rather subtle. He doesn't follow all of the Brooklyn accent "rules", such as pronouncing his "r"s like "ah"s (a Brooklyn accent would say "Mahk" instead of "Mark"). So, I suppose it's an accent that's more of his own, but it's close to the Brooklyn accent.

Scoefield was always inclined to speak this way because his mother had this kind of accent. After her death, he purposed to keep the accent so as to remember his mother and to keep her with him. Of course, after speaking this way constantly for years, this has become his permanent way of speaking. However, Scoefield remains very good at changing his voice and accent when he wants to.

Sarah doesn't have the accent simply because she doesn't necessarily want to. Speaking properly is more important to Sarah than it is to Scoefield. Moreover, the Scoefield accent wasn't prominent throughout the entire family. Amos Scoefield didn't have any accent and Sarah grew up without it as well.

7. Why did you put so many Bible passages in Scoefield? They tend to make the story drag a bit. Will this continue in the next books?

I am aware that I may have overdone it with the Bible passages in Henry and Sarah's devotion times/Pastor Benson's sermon. However, I wouldn't change it. Part of what arose out of my original ideas for Scoefield was that it could be used to educate and teach on the Bible, not just talk about someone who knew the Bible. It's part of what makes the Scoefield series stand out from the typical novel series, if you ask me. So yes, it will continue in the books to come. That being said, I do realize that it slows the overall plot down quite a bit if I lay down entire books of the Bible/entire sermons in them. So, I have made sure to trim a great deal of the Bible passages/sermons so as to not overload readers. It will still convey the message that is needed, but hopefully won't make the reader feel like he or she is wading through a Bible commentary to get to the next chapter.

8. Why make a 2nd Edition to Scoefield? Was it just to add bonus content and make more money?

Ooh, this one is going to hurt my pride a bit. No, the 2nd Edition was not just to add bonus content, nor is it just to get more sales (though more sales are appreciated). In all truthfulness, the 1st Edition to Scoefield had some major errors in it and the 2nd Edition was primarily made to correct them. See, I, like a dummy, threw away my original manuscript after I published the first version. But give me some slack, it was my first published book! I had no idea what I was doing.

In my flawed thinking, I thought "I published it! I don't need the manuscript anymore! It'll just take up more space on my computer!" and poof, I deleted it. About two seconds after I did that, my wife said to me "Why did you do that? You'll need that in case you need to fix any errors". In my hubris, I thought there were no errors. **WRONG!** A ton of errors were found! And now I had no manuscript to fix them with. So the entire book had to be rewritten in order to rectify some pretty big imperfections:

Major Error #1: "Boulder" Hat – When Henry and Sarah meet Mr. Butters, it is noted that he wears a "boulder" hat. But there is no such thing as a "boulder" hat. I just had mistakenly heard it as a "boulder" hat when it was really called a "bowler" hat. It's the kind of hat that Laurel and Hardy wear. Regardless, every time it mentioned Mr. Butters' hat, I had wrongly put it as a "boulder" hat instead of correctly calling it a "bowler" hat.

Major Error #2: Chapter Fifteen – Another grave mistake that came out of the original version was the heading for Chapter Fifteen. For whatever reason, the heading "Chapter Fifteen" ended up at the bottom of the last page of chapter fourteen. This gave the first page of chapter fifteen a wide, unnecessary gap at the top. A huge, glaring mistake. And it did the same for chapter sixteen and seventeen as well. I tried to fix it by editing the PDF that was used to print the Scoefield books, but was only successful in erasing all chapter headings from chapter fifteen and on. So, for chapter fifteen through seventeen, all chapter headings were missing. It just looked wrong altogether.

There were other errors, but those were the two most embarrassing and I told myself that I needed to fix them as soon as I could. Unfortunately, it took five years. But alas! They're gone now! And on top of that, I can add bonus material and make more money! But the biggest reason for a 2nd Edition was to correct mistakes. Moral of this story: never delete anything. Ever.

9. Why is it taking you so long to finish Blume?

That is not a Scoefield question, but I will answer it anyway. For those of you who don't know, Blume is the third book in the Scoefield series, coming after Engel. There are many reasons why it takes a good long while for me to get a book finished. First off, I am busy. I'm in the process of writing four books at the same time (not recommended). And for anyone who has a full-time job and a family, your days can get pretty packed on a consistent basis. My best writing times are either in the *very* early morning or in the dead of night. Neither of which are good for one's sleep schedule.

Secondly, the Scoefield series is hard to write. Why is that? Because it is realistic fiction/historical fiction. Everything that happens in it needs to be accurate to the times and to reality. I can't just come up with some sort of magic plant in order to fill in a plot-hole. Plus, that means I need to study the history thoroughly. A few of my readers are history buffs and I don't want to displease them anymore than I already have (if you're one of them, I apologize for the massive history mistake in Scoefield).

Thirdly, Blume is particularly hard for me. The theme (which will ***not*** be discussed any further here) needs to be handled in a very balanced manner, and it takes time and lots of editing to get that right.

Lastly, it needs to wait until three years after Engel. If you haven't noticed, there is a three year interval between each of the Scoefield books. Scoefield was published in 2017. Engel was published in 2020. Now, Blume is set to be published in 2023. The "rhyming" of the three year interval is very satisfying to me.

10. Why did you put sexual content in Scoefield? Wasn't that a bit on the inappropriate side for a Christian novel?

At the time of writing it, I was conflicted about putting it in there. Most of my readers are Christian men, women, boys, and girls that want to get away from that kind of junk in the world. After all, it's in movies, TV shows, magazines, etc. In America's culture, we are bombarded with it everywhere. And, honestly, the sexual content cost me from having Scoefield sold in a renowned Christian bookstore.

So why did I put it in there? Well, whether I failed or succeeded, it was to show the ugly side of immorality. The world and Hollywood display sex outside of marriage as fun, care-free, exciting, and wonderful. The truth is not so. There are countless examples of lives that were completely *ruined* because they decided to engage in sexual sin. And I felt that this culture needed to see that. Nothing good came out of Henry and Sarah's sin. They were already in love and Scoefield had given Henry permission to marry Sarah, so their marriage was not a product of their sexual sin. The only thing that Henry and Sarah ever received from that act was pain. Scoefield's friendship with Henry was shattered. Sarah was forced to choose between her love and her brother, which would bring agony no matter what she decided. And it marred God in the eyes of Scoefield because Henry was really the only example of Christianity that Scoefield knew. Let me say this again: sexual sin brought Henry and Sarah ***nothing good***.

Sexual sin is shown as so glamorous and lovely in our culture, but that's all a lie. Now, there may be some who say "But there was something good that came out of ***my*** sexual sin". Then thank the Lord, because He was able to take your mess and make something good come out of it. This can be likened to David and Bath-sheba's sin. They got Solomon out of something that began in sin. That was God's graciousness. But what else did they get? Bath-sheba lost her husband, Uriah, and her firstborn son. David was punished with evil that would arise out of his own house (Amnon and Absalom). Insurmountable pain on both ends. Was the fleeting moments of pleasure really worth years of regret? No. And it is still the same today.

So, was the sexual content inappropriate? Perhaps, though I tried to keep it as decent as I could while still conveying what happened. But I believe it was worth the risk. Because promiscuity is rampant in our culture and people need to wake up to the dangers, woes, and evils it causes. And, for the record, Scoefield is not a children's book. I don't believe anyone below twelve years of age should be reading it, since it deals with very real and difficult life situations. Engel is no different and neither will Blume be.

Forgive Me Once Again Sheet Music

Of all the songs that are in Scoefield, I was able to actually get one down on sheet music. Confession: I am *not* a composer. These little two pages were the result of several years of work. More importantly, I wouldn't have been able to actually compose this song without the invaluable help from a good friend of mine, Josiah Rice. All that being said, I do hope it brings some amount of joy to Scoefield fans to see that there is one of Henry's songs that does actually come with a tune. I do apologize that I couldn't line up the words with the sheet music (not tech savvy in the slightest. It's a miracle I was able to get the sheet music at all), but I imagine you'll be able to match up the words to the notes without much issue. Enjoy!

Forgive Me Once Again

Music and lyrics by Josiah Rice and Nicholas M. Krohn

Copyright 2022

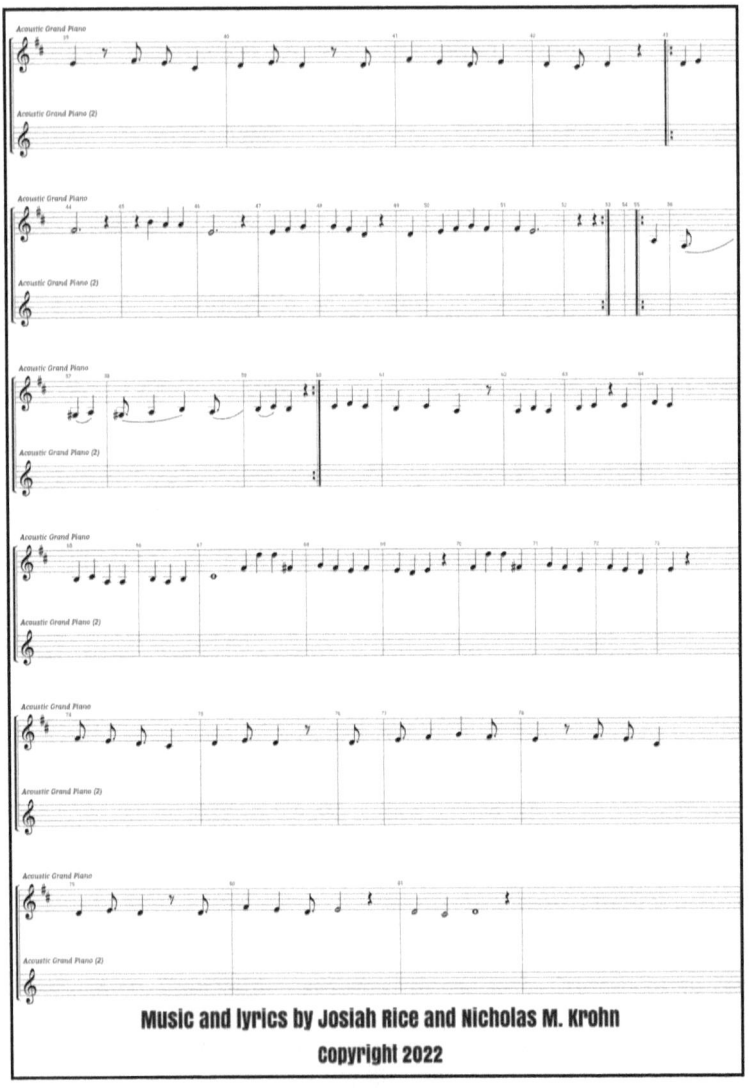

Music and lyrics by Josiah Rice and Nicholas M. Krohn
copyright 2022

254

Praise for 'Scoefield'

"A 'merry-go-round' of emotions. For me, it's a much needed reminder that Christians need always to maintain and keep our testimonies, and that the world is watching for us to mess up. I look forward to reading what new things we'll unravel."

– Adam S.

"The best part of this story and Scoefield himself are owed to the struggles we all face: the want for happiness, the need to provide for those we love, and what that means for the sanctity of the soul. Even at their lowest, the struggles of Henry Engel and Scoefield serve to highlight the truth that lies at the center of it all: that God provides."

–Andre T.

"Very good. I do like your analysis of (the Bible passages). They make it easier for people who don't know God to understand what each passage says. It answers very important questions that I've heard from many people who aren't saved in a clear and concise way."

–Kaylinn T.

Note to the Reader

Dear Reader,

As you've read through this book, you've probably noticed how much of the story centers around Christianity. Now, I don't know what you particularly feel about Christianity, but I would like to say something, if that's all right. What I am about to tell you does not come from a heart that is holier-than-thou or just wanting you to join my church. I tell you this because I am concerned for your soul. It's similar to a man at a beach that sees a shark in the water. Some of those who are swimming in the ocean don't notice the danger. So what should he do? Make them aware of the danger by yelling "SHARK!" And that's what I'm endeavoring to do. I want to warn you of the danger that's coming at the end of your life.

Recently, there have been a decent amount of people I have known that suddenly passed away. Most were unexpected and very shocking. It reminded me of a rather depressing truth: death is coming for all of us. We don't know when and we don't know how, but death will eventually come. And, for some, I kept thinking to myself "Where are they now?" I didn't know some of their faiths or beliefs. But I believe in a God that made the heavens and the earth. I believe that, in the beginning, the world was perfect. I believe that mankind sinned against God, thus shattering the perfection of creation. I believe that all have sinned and are worthy of judgment. I believe that Jesus Christ, God in human flesh, lived a sinless life and died on the cross so He might pay the price of our sin for us. I believe that anyone who calls upon Him will be saved from a literal, eternal hell. And I, as one of His believers, am to go out and tell others of His salvation so that they can be saved as well.

In today's age, there are thousands of faiths that someone can believe in. And people flock to religions because we, as humanity, have an inner knowledge that there is something bigger than all of us that first brought everything into being. Even atheists know that a higher being exists out there. They just choose to reject it. When my friends died, it forced me to think of their eternal destination. Their opportunity to choose is past and they are either in heaven with the Lord, or burning in the penetrating darkness of hell. This is not the most cheery stuff, I admit. But, as I said earlier, I'm concerned for your eternal destination. And I don't want anyone to go to hell. I wouldn't wish that on my worst enemy. So, if you'll permit me, I'd like to tell you about how you can get away from the shark, so to speak. Now, before I get into it, I will let you know that I'm not trying to make you my disciple or anything. I'm not trying to get accolades for converting someone to Christianity, and I'm most certainly not trying to force you become a Christian against your will. No, I'm telling you about it so you can make the choice for yourself. From my perspective, people are in grave danger. And, again, we don't know when our life will end. So what kind of person would I be if I believed in a real place called hell, but never told anyone how to be rescued from it?

So, without further ado, I'd like to lay out the steps of salvation, if that's all right with you.

1. <u>God is holy and cannot be in the presence of sin.</u>
"For I am the LORD that bringeth you up out of the land of
Egypt, to be your God: ye shall therefore be holy, for I am
holy."
Leviticus 11:45

"There is none holy as the LORD: for there is none beside
Thee: neither is there any rock like our God."
1 Samuel 2:2

"Holy, holy, holy, Lord God Almighty, which was, and is,
and is to come."
Revelation 4:8b

Holy is a word that means "set apart", "morally
blameless", or "sacred". Essentially, it means to be without
sin. Since God is holy, associating with sin would nullify
His holiness. It's like mixing oil with water or trying to put
light and darkness together. It can't happen. If God and
humanity are going to be in each other's presence, one of
them needs to change. And it's not going to be God.

2. <u>Every human is a sinner. Even the tiniest sin makes you incapable of being in God's presence and worthy of His wrath.</u>

"For all have sinned, and come short of the glory of God;"

Romans 3:23

This is where some believe that they are "good enough" with God because they haven't committed the big sins like murder, rape, etc., but if you think that, just look at the Ten Commandments and ask yourself "Have I broken any of these?":

1. Thou shalt have no other gods before Me.

2. Thou shalt not make unto thee any graven image.

3. Thou shalt not take the name of the LORD thy God in vain.

4. Remember the sabbath to keep it holy.

5. Honor thy father and mother.

6. Thou shalt not kill.

7. Thou shalt not commit adultery.

8. Thou shalt not steal.

9. Thou shalt not bear false witness.

10. Thou shalt not covet.

People usually acknowledge that they've broken at least one of the Ten Commandments (usually the one that deals with lying, at least). But, in the New Testament, Jesus added a higher standard with a few of these commandments. He said that if you held anger in your heart towards someone, you've committed murder in your heart. He also said if you look upon someone with lust who is not your spouse, you're committing mental adultery (adultery here is actually referring to sexual sin in general, not necessarily the specific act of cheating on a spouse, though that is included). Now, most people have done those things as well, which makes them lying, murdering adulterers. And that's just three of the Ten Commandments. But even if someone had only broken one little aspect of God's law, the New Testament also says this:

"For whosoever shall keep the whole law, and yet offend in one point, he is guilty of all."
James 2:10

It's like having a string tied to a ball. The string has ten knots in it, representing the Ten Commandments. If someone were to cut the knots with scissors, how many would they have to cut before the ball hits the ground? Just one. The same is true with God's law. If you just broke only one part of it, you're guilty. You're a sinner. And you cannot be in His presence. Thankfully, that's not where it ends.

3. <u>Sin leads to spiritual death, but Christ leads to spiritual life. The spiritual death will separate sinners from God to eternal hell. But Jesus paid the penalty so we can go to heaven.</u>

"But God commendeth His love toward us, in that, while we were yet sinners, Christ died for us."

Romans 5:8

"For the wages of sin is death; but the gift of God is eternal life through Jesus Christ our Lord."

Romans 6:23

A price needed to be paid because of humanity's sin. It can be likened to someone committing a crime of property damage. Someone has to pay for to repair the damage. But let's say it wasn't just any property that was damaged. Say it was something incredibly valuable, like the Eiffel Tower. If someone destroyed the Eiffel Tower, that would probably cost millions of dollars to replace. A price that most people cannot pay. When it comes to sin, the cost was even higher. Humanity in of itself could not pay for the cost of redemption. We needed someone to pay the debt for us. That someone is Jesus Christ. He paid the price by being a sacrifice for humanity. He is God, which means He is perfect and able to pay the cost for sin. But He is also man, because only a man could redeem mankind. His innocent blood was shed in order to give everyone an opportunity to be forgiven of their debt.

4. <u>Repent and place faith in Jesus. Believe that Jesus is the Son of God and claim the gift of eternal salvation that He offers you freely.</u>

"For God so loved the world, that He gave His only begotten Son, that whosoever believeth in Him should not perish, but have everlasting life."

John 3:16

"Repent ye therefore, and be converted, that your sins may
be blotted out, when the times of refreshing shall come
from the presence of the Lord;"
Acts 3:19.

"That if thou shalt confess with thy mouth the Lord Jesus,
and shalt believe in thine heart that God hath raised Him
from the dead, thou shalt be saved."
Romans 10:9

This sounds too simple to a lot of people. But Jesus already did all of the work for us. All we need to do is accept the gift. Imagine that we are all on death row, but a pardon has been offered to everyone. All we need to do is accept the pardon and we're set free. But we have the choice to also refuse the pardon. In history, there have been people placed on death row that were given a pardon from the president, yet they refused and were put to death anyway. The same is true for spiritual salvation. You can refuse it. But the consequence is eternal hell.

Again, I want to make it crystal clear that I'm not trying to force any of this upon you. I'm simply telling you this because I believe it to be true and I don't want you to suffer a terrible fate of going to hell when you die. Now, I realize that this is not always what people want to hear, but you must understand my motives and that they are not malicious or deceptive in any sense. And I hope this hasn't come across as judgmental or unfeeling. I promise that is not my heart behind this. As a Christian, it is at the core of my belief that all people are bound for hell without Jesus Christ's gift of salvation. And I don't want you to suffer in hell for all eternity. I would like to see you in heaven someday.

Sincerely,
Nicholas M. Krohn.

About the Author

Nicholas M. Krohn has always had a love for both writing and the Lord. Nicholas received Jesus Christ as his Lord and Saviour at the age of nine, thanks to his faith-filled mother and a godly church. After his salvation, Nicholas spent most of his childhood free-time jotting down fantastical stories. When he was a teenager, Nicholas discovered that writing was his calling from God. When attending Heartland Baptist Bible College, Nicholas began seriously writing and self-publishing novels with the desire that they would both wholesomely entertain readers, yet bring glory to God's name. It was here that he met his wife, Marissa, whom he married in 2017 (and who is an invaluable part of Nicholas' writing process by means of cover art, editing, inspiration, and simply saying "That doesn't make sense" when certain ideas are thrown at her). Halfway through college, Nicholas also realized that he could do more than just write Christian Fiction. After deep study in the Bible and graduating from Heartland Baptist Bible College in 2020, Nicholas made it his mission to not only point to the Lord with his fiction novels, but to expound on the Word of God itself through commentaries, in-depth studies, and other such works of literature. Nicholas continues to pursue this work while living in Iowa with his wife and children.

OTHER KROHN'STORIES BOOKS

(All available on Amazon)

MARISSA KROHN

The Silent Princess (*Children's book*)

NICHOLAS M. KROHN

BIBLE COMMENTARY SERIES

Krohn's Commentary of the First Book of Samuel

Krohn's Commentary of the Second Book of Samuel

THE SCOEFIELD SERIES (*HISTORICAL FICTION*)

Scoefield

Engel

Blume

THE ZALIAN CHRONICLES (*CHRISTIAN FANTASY*)

Heroes & Thieves I: The Noble Bandit

Heroes & Thieves II: A Bundle of Fools

Heroes & Thieves III: Clapia's Rebirth

Heroes & Thieves IV: Two Wastelands

KROHN'S STORIES POETRY
Trains, Bridges, Cups, & Cheese
The Rambling of a Cart Pusher

CONTACT US
Website: krohnstories.storiad.com
Facebook Group: Krohn'Stories Books
Instagram: krohnstoriesbooks
Email: krohnstories@gmail.com
Fan mail, inquiries, suggestions, and critiques are all welcome. We will do our best to reply to all messages/emails, but cannot promise due to a busy schedule. Please be appropriate. Any swearing, vulgarity, threatening, or otherwise inappropriate messages/emails will be deleted without any response.